DEVIL
YOU KNOW

USA TODAY BESTSELLING AUTHORS

J.L. BECK &
C. HALLMAN

1

NIC

*M*y father used to say: a man doesn't wait around for what he wants, he goes out, and he takes it. An ideology I live my life by. When I want power, I create it. When I want money, I get it. When I want revenge... nothing will stand in my way.

Doubt has no place in my life. So why is it creeping up my spine like a fucking disease today? Why is the idea of handing Celia over to the man who bought her turning my stomach?

There is an invisible rope wrapped around my neck, and with every inch I move further away from Celia, that rope tightens, strangling me. I step into a side hallway to collect my thoughts and catch my breath. The rope refuses to loosen, no matter how much I reason with myself.

Every second I waver is uncertain. And uncertainty gets you killed.

I square my shoulders and head off to find Soo. He's handling the money; he can also handle Celia's transfer. I'm not sure I could go through with it if I was the one that had to do it. Call me a coward, but I couldn't follow through with this if I saw her face again.

Most of the bidders are still crowding around the main warehouse space. The heavy tang of cigar smoke coats the air so thick you can taste it. Tucked in the back of the room is a glass window. On the other side of that is the room where Soo waits and watches for someone to do something stupid. When I enter, he's at his terminal, set against the wall to the right of the doorway, watching the cameras, monitoring every angle.

I step inside his sanctum and lean against his desk. "You handle the transfer?"

Soo nods. "I've just finalized payment. All that remains is the physical exchange."

His long fingers stroke over the keyboard as he finishes typing the sales sheet, then he stands, walks across the room, and grabs a mound of silver chains from the floor. On one end is a spiked choke collar made for a dog. Acid rises up my throat, burning me from the inside out.

"What the fuck is that?"

Soo shrugs, shouldering the chains. They clank together, and the sound grates on my already frayed nerves. "The buyer requested her to wear these, and only these, when I hand her over to him."

The sounds of the crowd narrow to the clink of those chains. Each individual link swaying over his arm.

I allow myself a flash of what they would look like draped over her naked skin, the collar around her slender neck, and white-hot rage pricks at me. The chains must weigh twenty pounds at least. Not only would they bruise her delicate skin, but they would be heavy and hard for her to manage.

Causing my princess discomfort isn't something I shy from. But there's a difference between cruelty and control. Dominance and depravity.

I'm selling her to some dickhole who will use her body until it breaks and then throw her away. I knew this... I knew that her fate was sealed. Fuck! I sealed it myself. I prepared myself for this, promising that I wouldn't falter. But knowing something will happen and being in that moment are two different things.

I thought I could push my feelings aside for my revenge. I thought I could ignore my conscience and forget she ever existed. Instead, I feel like I'm being torn apart, my insides shredded into a million pieces. There is a gaping hole in my chest, bleeding me dry, and there's only one way to stop the bleeding.

"Put the chains down, Soo. You won't touch her with them."

Soo drops the chains without a word. They hit the floor with a dull thud. He doesn't get the chance to ask questions because I'm already marching to the office where we stashed her to wait.

Doubt has no place in my life. So, I'll cut it out and take Celia home where she belongs, with me.

Once the decision is made in my mind, it lifts an invisible weight off my shoulders. I know I made the right choice, and if any man dares to touch her, I'll rip off his hands and cut them into tiny pieces before feeding them to him bit by bit. Celia is mine, and I'm going to make it crystal fucking clear to her and everyone else from now on.

With each step I take, the clench of my jaw loosens, and the grinding of my teeth stops altogether. Her buyer better stay the fuck out of my way, or he'll be the first one to die tonight.

My insides are a twisted mess by the time I reach the door to the office. I do my best to mask my features. I don't want her to know that she's gotten to me, not even a little bit.

Taking the brass doorknob in my hand, I twist and find it locked. I shouldn't be surprised. Of course, my minx is doing everything possible to stop the sale from going through. Little does she know she's not going home with anyone but me. I jiggle the handle, and with a heavy exhale, I dig into my pocket for the key. The seconds it takes to unlock the door are too long. With more effort than necessary, I shove it open and immediately seek the sheen of her dark hair, the tight curve of her waist, the creamy pale skin I want to taste.

The noise from the crowd makes it hard to hear, so I step further into the room, scanning every corner and exit. The hair on the back of my neck rises when I realize she's not here. She's not in the fucking room.

CELIA FUCKING ESCAPED. *Again.* I clench my jaw, adding to the ache there, doing another scan to be sure she's not hiding somewhere.

The room is empty. My anger toward her rises with every single second that passes. The moment I find her, I'm going to take it out on her pretty little ass. She won't be able to walk for a fucking week, especially not once I have her tied to the bed.

Soo enters the room behind me, pausing mid-motion, taking in the empty room as well. "Did you already move her?"

Jaw clenched, I reply, "No, I fucking didn't."

There are no windows and only one other entrance across the space we mostly use for storage. Technically, it's an office, but there's only a desk, a small lamp, and boxes of alcohol brought in for the auction.

Soo marches across the room to the other door, throws it open, and pokes his head out. "I'd be pretty impressed if she got out of here on her own. To get past that crowd, and me, with no one seeing a thing. It's very unlikely."

I peer around the room again. "You think she had help? Or that someone helped themselves?"

He doesn't answer, just slips into the hall, probably returning to his computer to bring up the video feeds throughout the warehouse. We keep the inside, and the outside, covered. There are very few blind spots in this place.

I head out the door nearest me, cutting through the throng of men. I don't make it far before a small tan man grabs my arm.

With a jerk, I pull my arm back and turn, taking a step toward him. "Excuse me," I growl, barely hanging onto my control.

The noise of these men is too much, the clinking of glasses, the smoke, all of it is more than I can take while I'm imagining someone else with their hands on what's mine.

"Mr. Diavolo, you have something that belongs to me. I'd like to take her home now."

I stare down at the man and recognize him as the one who bought Celia. The one who wants to clothe her in chains.

I narrow my gaze, questioning the man, "Are you sure she belongs to you?"

His bushy eyebrows pop up at such an accusation. "I don't appreciate your game, sir. I wish to leave."

I wave at the door to the warehouse. I'm losing my mind, losing it all because a beautiful fucking woman wove her way into my black soul. "Then go."

The men around me continue on with their charades, laughing and tipping back bourbon. Drinking on my dollar. Anger flares, threatening to burn me to the ground if I don't extinguish it. The problem is, I don't care if I burn or if I burn the entire world down with me. Not if I can't find her. Raising my voice above the crowd, I yell, "All of you, get the fuck out."

Soo rushes to my side, whispering in my ear. "We'll find her. Calm down. You're going to blow everything up in our faces."

"Don't tell me to fucking calm down and don't tell me what to fucking do. I'm in charge here."

Soo turns to the crowd, stepping between me and the man that bought Celia. "Thank you all for coming. We are wrapping up early tonight. Please finish your drinks and head to your vehicles."

"Not without my property," Celia's buyer growls.

I take a threatening step forward, ready to bash his little brains into the side of a crate, when Soo once again interferes. "Go back to my office. I'll handle this."

"You better because you don't want to know what's going to happen if I do."

It takes everything within me to simply clench my fists and not batter my best friend for getting in my way. Sensing my behavior and rage, Soo adds, "If you want to go head-to-head, we can, but not until I clear this place out."

Instead of answering, I spin on my heels and go back to his office. On the way, I throw a half-empty bottle of bourbon against a stack of crates. It shatters satisfyingly, barely curbing my rage, causing those around it to skitter away from the glass and me.

The destruction doesn't help as I walk into the office. A storm is raging inside my head, in my chest. She's already escaped once, so I wouldn't put it past her to leave again. But Soo is also right. There's no way she walked out of here without help or coercion. Celia is smart, but I seriously doubt she'd be able to pull this off on her own. So, the question remains, did she get help, or was she stolen?

Both thoughts send me into another tailspin of anger. Clenching my fists, I press them into Soo's countertop, letting the cold from the stone sink into my skin. Of course, it doesn't help. I just need a minute to rein in the heat coating my bones, the need to destroy, to burn, to kill anyone standing between her and me.

The noise of the crowd is dimming, and the air stirs behind me as Soo enters.

"What the hell was that?" he demands, his tone hard.

He's the only man in the world who can speak to me like that, but he better tread lightly because I'm still on the edge of slamming his head into the granite beneath my hands.

"I think someone took her. Despite how angry she is at me or how much she hates me, I doubt she'd have been able to escape on her own."

The click of Soo's keyboard keys garners my attention. He's pulled up the cameras from every angle, and his eyes glide between each one, inspecting them for any clues. "I don't see her in any of these frames."

I move behind him and stare at the screen, hunting for a flash of red, her glossy dark hair, anything, but I see nothing but rich assholes drinking too much. Even on the outside camera feed, there is nothing.

"Where the fuck did she go? How could someone steal her without us noticing?"

Soo's brow furrows, his wheels spinning. "No one could unless they know where our cameras are."

I jab at the keyboard. "Pull it all up, everything we have from your arrival until right this fucking moment."

Soo's fingers move quickly, loading the monitors with every camera angle. At least a dozen of them. "You know we don't have time for this. The five families should know by now that we were auctioning one of theirs off. They will probably act swiftly. Maybe even make a move tonight, a possible emergency meeting. We need to focus on them, watch and be prepared to strike at any moment."

His words cut through some of the fog in my brain. "I need to find her."

"You won't get another chance like this," Soo reminds me cautiously.

The rage boils over. Of course, he is right, but I can't seem to care. "Do I look like I give a shit right now? I want you to fucking find her! I want you to stop trying to manage my rage. If I want to kill someone, I will, and nothing you say will stop me."

Before I take a swipe at the computers helping us, I pound my fist into the doorframe. The solid wood doesn't give, and pain shoots up my arm from the contact. I let myself breathe it in, assimilate it, allow it to beat back the monster. I'm not calm, but I'm not in danger of killing Soo, which is the point of my bruised knuckles.

The doubt I've been fighting creeps back in under my defenses, wiggling through the resolve I've latched on to. What if I can't find her? What if the person who stole her is closer than I think? If someone can slip her out without either of us seeing, without even registering on the cameras, then they work on the inside of my organization, or they've been watching us for a long time. The idea of someone who works alongside me betraying me, stealing what is mine, intensifies my rage.

"Find her, Soo," I grate, staring down at the blood welling across the already purple ridges of my knuckles.

As I expect, he says nothing but continues typing at a furious pace while his eyes track across the six monitors mounted above his desk.

When the ticks stop, I swing around and study the screens. "What is it?"

Soo points to one screen, where a white van is parked near the back exit. It's usually locked during events, so people can't sneak in behind us. A figure dressed in black, hood up, exits the van and walks right in the back door.

I rush out into the main warehouse and charge toward the door. It's closed, and when I shove it open, it glides outward and slams into the wall behind with a heavy thump.

"Motherfucker."

Soo peeks out the door from beside me. "I take it you didn't unlock it."

"No, you?"

He shakes his head and goes back to his terminal. I follow and watch as he fast forwards through the feed. A little while after the van parks, a figure exits the building with a large black bag slung over his shoulder. He loads the bag into the back of the van and slams the door. Then goes around to the driver's side, climbs in, and pulls away.

"What time did he arrive?" I point to the monitor of the driveway up to the warehouse.

Soo patters on his keys some more and loads the van arriving. It was right as the auction started. The bastard saw the event, decided not to bid, and then stole her right from under our noses.

I spin and take another shot at the doorframe. My knuckles scream, the pain once again cuts through some of my rage.

"Figure out who he is," I order.

Soo says nothing, already working his magic. He types furiously, and I wait, the time ticking through me a second at a time. Each amping me higher and higher.

When he stops again, I turn and focus on the screens. One image fills all six screens. It's an angled shot of the van, arriving at the event, through the windshield. It's dark. The face and head of the man are concealed, but his hands, gripping the wheel, are bare. He must have put gloves on before he entered the building. It's obvious he was trying to cover his tracks.

But there's no hiding what I see on his right hand. Clear as day, perched at noon on the steering wheel, is the word *'hate'* tattooed across his knuckles. All-consuming dread fills my stomach. While anyone on Earth could have a tattoo like that, I know of only one man.

The one man who's been missing through this entire operation.

Fucking Lucas.

2

CELIA

*M*y head aches. It's the kind of ache you get from being out all night making indecent decisions. The pain radiates from the back of my skull forward like some macabre crown. It wreathes my senses.

I blink my eyes open to stare at a high, white ceiling with delicate crown molding skirting the edges. It's dark, but there's light filtering from my left, like a lamp that was left on in another room.

I let my eyes flutter closed and drift into a middle space, a dreamy place where the pain ebbs and flows instead of being in a constant state. When I open my eyes again, I shift to the side, pressing my face into a soft white pillow. I lift my head and peer down at the sheets underneath me, they're white, and the blanket at my feet is a deep navy. I sit up and look around the room, trying to make out what little I can through the dim light leaking in.

There's a bedside table, a minimalist piece, with a stainless-steel lamp on it.

Beside it, an alarm clock blinks red numbers back at me. Four a.m.

The memory of the night before breaks up the headache. Images flicker through my mind. Me sitting on Nicolo's lap. The stupid red dress, which as I look down at myself, I realize I'm still wearing. Him threatening me after he fucking sold me.

He fucking sold me. Disgust churns low in my gut. The bastard actually did it. That's the only thing sticking out in my mind right now. His angry face looming over mine, his cruel words, his eyes saying goodbye.

I sit up, dragging air into my lungs, panic creeping in. I can't believe he fucking sold me. I look around the room, wondering where the hell I am. Is this my buyer's home? I listen, focusing the best I can around the raging heartbeat pounding in my ears. *Nothing.* Silence surrounds me. There isn't a single sound to break up the noise.

Gingerly, I push off the bed. My bare feet sink into a shaggy rug. When I can stand upright, I wobble toward the doorway.

Stepping out of the room, I find there is a lamp on a side table near a long black leather couch. There's art on the wall above it, a big flat screen opposite, and a balcony beyond. I'm so high up, I can see the tips of skyscrapers lighting up the dark in the distance. Knowing how high up I am, there is no escaping from a window. My only option is the door.

I head toward it, past a large kitchen and another doorway. My fingers shake as I grasp the knob in my hand. One twist is all it takes to discover it's locked. Someone locked me inside this house.

But who? When I try to remember, it just spurs the headache on, the damn thing raking its claws through my brain.

I turn back to the room and scan the décor again. If I can't find a way out, maybe I can find a weapon. My eyes touch on the block of knives sitting on the countertop. I rush into the kitchen and whip out the biggest one I can get my hands on. Whoever's holding me captive is an idiotic man. With the knife heavy in my hand, I walk back into the living room. Having a weapon makes me feel better, but I need to know more about who purchased me.

From the living room, I head back into the bedroom, flicking on the light as I go. Looking around the room, I locate a closet tucked in the far side of the room. I cross the space and throw the doors open. The inside is stuffed with men's clothing, all in shades of black and gray. There is everything from jeans to suits, giving me no distinct variation of who this man might really be. I feel like a hamster on a wheel, going nowhere.

I drop my gaze to the floor with defeat, and that's when I see it—a scrap of champagne silk. I grab the end that's showing and pull it out from underneath a pair of dirty boots. With the fabric in my hands, I stare at it. The memories swarm me. The night Nicolo took me, sitting on a mattress in the basement, wearing this, and Lucas, Nic's brother, walking out with it clutched in his huge fist.

Lucas. Again, the memories rush back in, and I recall him coming into the room at the auction. Him knocking me out after saying he's my... *what?* His words are a haze.

My knees give out from pure exhaustion, and I sink to the plush carpet of the walk-in closet. A spicy scent permeates the space—like a deodorant or a cologne, not laundry soap. I don't remember smelling it before, but then again, I didn't consider Lucas like I did Nicolo. Whenever Nicolo walked into a room, all my focus shifted to him. Prey waiting to be torn apart by the stronger predator.

I don't know how long I sit staring down at the silk fabric, but it's long enough that my legs ache from the awkward angle. I notice the knife sitting beside me on the carpet, and I don't even remember dropping it.

A heavy metallic thud, followed by a sharp clicking noise, drags me back to the present. I grab the blade and scramble underneath the pile of clothes, using them to hide behind. The sound had definitely been the lock, right? Or maybe I'm going crazy.

My heartbeat thunders in my ears, and the pain biting around the back of my skull intensifies as I struggle to quiet my breathing.

Footsteps crunch on the carpet as they come into the room. There is a pause, and I hold my breath as he opens what I assume is the bathroom door before moving oto the closet door.

The light flicks on, illuminating the small space, and I can't hold my breath anymore, so I release it slowly, carefully, modulated. It doesn't matter, though.

"I know you're in here, Celia. Now get your ass out here, because I don't feel like chasing you down. I have food, water, and clothing for you."

It's the last one that drives me to step out of my hiding spot. I peek out from between his suits. Lucas stands before me, dressed in black from head to toe. My memory wasn't warped. He really kidnapped me, but the question remains... why?

"Give me the clothes and let me change, and I'll come out."

He rolls his eyes and tosses something on the floor. I snatch up the pile, watching him like a snake that could strike at any given time. When he shuts the door to the bedroom, I crawl out from my hiding spot and look at what he brought.

A pair of black leggings, underwear, and an oversized T-shirt sit inside a plastic bag. If I wasn't so mad and confused, I would probably rejoice about this new wardrobe. It's my first official set of clothing since being kidnapped.

I quickly put the clothes on, tossing the dress in the back of the closet, and exit, knife in hand along my thigh.

Lucas is in the kitchen, pulling white Chinese food containers from a paper bag. A spicy scent reaches my nostrils, and my stomach lets out a loud rumble.

"Hungry?" Lucas asks like he didn't just hear my stomach and points to a stool on the other side of the counter.

I take the seat, but he doesn't do anything but stare at me. His expression deadpan, his eyes narrowing on me.

"What?"

He extends his hand out to me. "Knife. Then you can have this chicken and rice."

To give up my weapon is a trap, and I clutch the knife tighter, but my stomach betrays me further, rumbling in protest. With a sigh, I slam the knife down on the countertop and hold out my empty hand for the food box.

Lucas shakes his head and returns the knife to the block on the opposite counter. I watch him warily as he places a box in front of me, a pair of wooden chopsticks on top. Before he can change his mind, I snap the box up, rip open the top, and dig into the food—spicy chicken on a bed of white rice. The heat of the chicken pairs perfectly with the rice, and I have to keep my groan of appreciation locked down tight.

He leans against the opposite counter and digs into his own food. We eat in silence, which I'm thankful for. Once I polish off my food, he crosses the counter and slides an enormous bottle of water toward me. Again, I pounce on it and guzzle a huge amount of the liquid down just in case he tries to take it away.

No longer concerned with food, and a little sleepy, I study him. He looks like Nic in the eyes, but the rest of his features are different. His hair is much lighter, a sort of dirty blond. I think if it wasn't for his tattoo-covered skin and permanent frown, he would actually look a lot younger.

"Well, I'm here. Should I thank you for saving me from whatever fresh hell my buyer had in store? Or did you bring me here for your own perverse needs?"

His brows pull together, and his nose wrinkles in disgust. "I saved you for myself."

Ew. Not that he isn't a handsome man, but no way. He and I had never really hit it off back at the house. I can't imagine sex would help matters. Not that the Diavolo bastards ever consider giving me a choice in something.

"If it's all the same to you, I'd rather die than sleep with you."

I slide off the chair and back away from him, determined to fight this time. When I let Nicolo touch me and didn't fight, it felt different. Right here and now, all I feel is anger and pain. Nothing like the searing heat Nicolo somehow elicits from my body.

When his eyes narrow at me, his chopsticks halfway to his lips, I scramble to explain. "I know I might have thrown myself at you the other day, offered myself, but it was more about saving my skin from being sold than wanting to sleep with you." I backtrack a little, trying to maintain the peace.

If I've learned anything about Lucas, it's that he's a ticking time bomb waiting to detonate. "Not that you don't have your charms or anything. I just think we wouldn't be compatible. I'm sure there are plenty of women out there who would love to join your bed, but I'm just not in a great place after your fucking brother's handling. I can't even imagine sex with anyone, let alone you."

His disgust turns palpable as he drops his food into the sink, container, chopsticks, and all. "Did I do some damage when I knocked you on your little head?" He pauses. "I didn't bring you here to fuck you, Celia. I brought you here to talk to you. To get some answers without my brother breathing down my fucking neck."

Jesus Christ. My relief is a physical thing lying across my skin in a soothing veil. "Oh. Okay, well, I can answer questions, sure."

Lucas gives me a questioning look. "You don't remember what I told you when I retrieved you from the warehouse?"

So, we're using the word *'retrieved'* not kidnapped? Is that how Nicolo justifies his actions, too? These fucking men and their need to knock me out and transport me places against my will.

I narrow my eyes at him. "Some of it, maybe?" Thinking back now, I remember him speaking, but not exactly what he said.

He braces his big hands on the counter, tattoos etched on his knuckles. One hand says *'love,'* the other says *'hate.'* Charming. "I told you I was your fucking brother."

The world stops spinning, the floor falls beneath my feet, and it comes back to me now. Bit by bit, the pieces of my memory float down and back into place. The pulsing migraine I woke up with finally makes sense.

"You hit me."

"Is that any way to talk to your brother?" His words echo through my head.

No... the weight of his confession knocks the wind from my lungs.

"I didn't think you'd stay still while we escaped. I couldn't risk you drawing anyone's attention and getting us caught," he continues talking, but it's like his voice is far away now.

Brother. I blink, letting my mind digest what he's saying.

"You can't be my brother. You're lying. This is about control. You want to hurt me, just like your brother did. There is no way we are related." I take another step away from him.

"Trust me, I didn't want to believe it either, but we are. I have proof. We are one-hundred percent blood-related."

My knees give out, and I sink to the floor in a heap. *Brother.*

Oh. My. Fucking. God. I cover my face with my hands to slow my sudden need to drag in more air. Holy fuck. No.

I glance up at Lucas. His brows are drawn down as he studies me. It looks like he... Well, he cares, which is strange since I've never seen him show a shred of compassion toward anyone.

"Are you all right?"

"If you're my..." I bring my fingers to my mouth again, trying to re-order my thoughts into a sequence that makes sense. "If you're my brother, then... Nicolo?" I whisper his name. Even saying it now feels wrong, forbidden.

Catching on, he shakes his head heavily, a smile playing on his lips. "While I enjoy seeing your panic and fear, I won't get answers out of you if I drive you down a road like that. So, I'll just be honest. No, you're not related to Nic."

Something eases inside me, letting me go, until I slump forward against the countertop of his kitchen, my forehead pressed to the surface.

"Don't tell me I hit you too hard?" He speaks more to himself than me as he walks around the counter to loom over me. "I need you to answer some questions before you decide to check out."

I sit back up and then lumber to my feet just because I don't like him there staring down at me like that. "No, I'm fine. Just relieved is all. Your brother didn't care about using me for whatever he wanted." I don't bother keeping the bite from my tone.

He steps forward, crowding me. "Let's be clear. While I don't want to have sex with you, I have no problem carving you up to get the information I need. Blood might relate us, but we are not family. I'll kill you the same way I would kill any of my enemies."

I snort and retreat to the couch, sitting down at the very end. Lucas simply stares at me like he is waiting for a retort from me.

"What? Do you want me to refute that? My sister was my only family as far as I'm concerned."

Thankfully, he doesn't join me, only studies me, his arms crossed over his chest, making him appear even bigger in the already small space. "And your father?"

"What about him? He never really cared much about us since we were both girls and pretty much useless to him... other than marrying us off."

It's not the answer he wants. His brow furrows further, and he stares off over my shoulder.

"Just ask your questions, so I can get out of here."

He turns his gaze back to mine.

"Please?" I add, hoping it will buy me points.

When his eyes narrow again, I know it hasn't. But he doesn't speak. Instead, he goes back around the counter and digs into his food. *Awesome.* As talkative as his brother. These Diavolo men have brooding silences on lock.

While he eats, I consider his words. My brother. But how? He couldn't be more than a few years away from me in age. My parents tried for more children after me but never succeeded as far as I knew.

"How do you know? That you're my brother? In what way are we related? I mean, do we have the same father or mother?" I rattle off all my questions, daring to interrupt his meal for the sake of answers.

He finishes chewing and eyes me over his food container. "I took your slip the day Nic brought you to the house. I got your DNA tested with mine and with Nic's. You are only related to me, and since we were born the same year, it has to be on our father's side."

"So, who's our father, though?" The possibility of my father not being my actual father has actual hope blooming in my chest. It would explain so much, and it would be a lie to say I wouldn't be relieved.

"The man you grew up with is our biological father."

"How do you know?"

"I just do," he growls, making it clear he doesn't want to elaborate more on the subject.

"So, my father had an affair with your mother?"

His snort tells me what he thinks of that theory. "Sorry to disappoint you, but our father isn't just an asshole. He's also a rapist. He raped my mother, and she got pregnant with me."

The horror must be plain on my face because he laughs darkly and shovels more rice into his mouth.

"No, what... How?" My father is many things, and not all of them good I'm learning the longer I'm away from him, but a rapist? "How do you know?"

He narrows his eyes at me now. "Because my mother loved my father, and she wouldn't have cheated on him, especially not with a man like Ricci."

His using my family name jolts me. I close my eyes and try to compose myself.

"I think that's why he killed her. She wanted to reveal the truth. I didn't understand it at the time, but now everything makes sense. He called me a bastard son once in anger. My mother wanted everyone to know what he did, and that's what got my family slaughtered."

His words slowly sink into my brain. It takes me a few moments to make sense of it all, to wrap my head around it. Lucas is my half-brother. Why would he lie to me? He's kidnapped me and has me under his control. He doesn't need to lie to me to compound his ownership.

I have a brother, and my father is a rapist. Great, another fact I need to deal with. Another fact I can focus on once I've gained my freedom. "What do you want from me? Are you still dead set on revenge? You don't think your brother has handled that enough?"

He looks me right in the eyes. The darkness in his is terrifying, but I don't dare look away. The words roll off his tongue smoothly.

"I don't want revenge from you anymore, Celia. Now, I only want answers."

3

NIC

While Soo is very good at his job, he can't seem to find a record of Lucas's movements leading up to the auction. Which seems impossible since my fucking brother has never made any effort to shield his life from me before.

Why would he do this? The only answer that comes to mind is revenge. Me getting revenge against Ricci isn't enough for him; he wants his own taste. And maybe he thinks Celia can give him that or offer him a way to hit Ricci even harder.

I spin away from Soo's bank of computers and grab a liquor bottle from his bar. Not even bothering with a glass, I tip the bottle against my lips and take a long draft of the amber liquid.

"That's unsanitary," Soo says, still typing away at his computers.

For half a second, I savor what it would look like to throw the bottle against the screens, watch all that glass shatter and break on the floor. I'm not a man who loses control like this. I pride myself on control, but it seems Celia brings the worst out in me.

Even now, I want her body under my hands to both hold and destroy. To show her this rage eating me up from the inside out.

Soo works some magic on the screen and pulls up some maps. I replace the bottle and cross the room to stand behind his chair. "What am I looking at?"

On the screen is a smattering of red dots all over the city, in almost every corner. Soo points to the warehouse on the map and then the mansion. "Usually, Lucas's movements center around our main hubs. Even when we are busy and have to go out for shipments, he always ends up back at one of these two places. But this time, it's like he knows I'm tracking his phone, and he's purposefully made a pretty little map that shows us fuck all."

I wave at the map. "How long have you been tracking his phone? And why?"

Soo levels me a look. "Because your brother has been acting strangely. He's never where he's supposed to be these days, and he completely missed helping plan the event tonight. Now I guess I see why. He's been busy."

He has a point. Leading up to Celia's auction, I've barely seen Lucas, the last time being when I caught him and Celia together in my office. The image of her touching him shoots a new hole in the tattered remains of my control.

"What can we do about this mess? Can you remove his fake leads so we can see where he's been?"

Soo shakes his head. "No, I can't. We need more data to layer over this. It might help us narrow down his authentic movements better."

I fist my hands at my sides. "What kind of data? My patience is wearing thin."

"You think he'll hurt her?"

How can I possibly know what's inside my little brother's head? My brother is an enigma. He hides his pain, his rage, beneath layers of broken glass. There is no reaching him unless he wants you to reach him.

"I don't know. She represents revenge, and maybe he thinks he can get to Ricci on his own by using her?"

I brace my hands on the edge of his desk and grip the sturdy wood tighter in my grasp. "Help me, Soo, because if he hurts her, I'll fucking rip him apart. I'll tear this goddamn town to the ground if that's what it takes to find her."

No doubt sensing how close I am to snapping, Soo doesn't respond to that but goes in another direction. "Let's say he doesn't plan on hurting her. What do you think he wants with her then? What can Celia give him that required him to take her first, that he couldn't get out of her at the house during the time she was locked up there?"

I'd kept my brother away from her the best I could while she'd been my guest. Since the first night, he'd made it clear he wanted to kill her. In fact, had I not walked into that cell when I did, he would've snapped her neck. My heartbeat races against my ribs, and the blood swooshes in my ears. I have to find her, and standing here looking at fucking computer screens will not give me an answer. I strip my suit jacket off and throw it on Soo's counter. Then I roll my sleeves up to my forearms, grab the bottle of liquor, and walk out.

Of course, he follows me to the car and climbs into the driver's seat as I take the passenger side. "Where are we going?"

I take a swig of the liquor, letting it burn a path of angry fire down my throat. "To the house. If you can't get answers from his movements, we are going to see if we can get some information from his bedroom.

And if that doesn't work, I know at least one safe house he keeps in the city for when he's drug running."

Soo pulls away from the warehouse after a quick text to some of his men to clean up the space and lock everything down.

I stare out the window, cradling the bottle in my lap, but I don't drink any more, no matter how tempting it might be. The drive is the longest twenty minutes of my life, and I spend the majority of the time with my thoughts circling around if Celia is dead.

Could I kill my brother? Would I? When we get to the house, I leave the bottle on the side table. If—when—we find Celia, I can't be drunk off my ass. Especially as I rip my little brother to pieces for taking what's mine.

I march down the long hallway to his room, where the door is cracked open. Using my foot, I send the heavy cedar door back against the wall and survey the room. It's clean, which is strange considering how unkempt the man usually is. Soo dives right in, digging through drawers and under his mattress. Not all that surprising. The entire place is spotless, like he barely even lives here, and I guess in a way he doesn't. My hands clench into tight fists involuntarily. The rage simmers low in my veins. No, this isn't where he would keep something he doesn't want me to find.

I walk out of the room, and it only takes a couple of seconds for Soo to be on my heels. We head down to the garage, and I make a straight shot to the motorcycle he loves more than anything else in the world. Soo gets there before I do, maybe to ensure I don't destroy it.

"Check the seat. He's probably got something we can use in there. If he wanted to hide something, it would be in there or at one of his safe houses."

Soo nods and riffles through the seat compartment. After a few seconds, he draws out a bedraggled stack of papers, scans them, and hands them to me. "This might help. It seems your brother has become quite the real estate entrepreneur."

Each of the five pages is a layout of an apartment in town. The addresses printed neatly in the corners. None of them is the one I know of him having, which means there are six locations we need to check.

I crumple the pages in my hand, and a red-hot haze engulfs me. We'll never get to them all tonight, which gives him more time to enact his plan, whatever the fuck that might be. "Who do we have out there? Start texting your sources. Get them monitoring these addresses until we find out which one is in use."

Soo closes the motorcycle seat and drags his phone from his pocket. I hand over the papers, and in under three minutes, he has men out watching all the listed addresses. "Do you think he would prefer one over any other?" he asks.

I snap. "How the fuck should I know? Apparently, I don't know a thing about the asshole," I yell, my voice echoing through the garage.

The rational part of my brain knows Soo is helping me, that this isn't his fault, and yet he's the only safe outlet to this anger consuming me right now. But it's not just anger, it's fear, and I hate it. I hate it so much. Fear has zero place in my life, and somehow the idea of something happening to Celia sends it into overdrive.

"I highly doubt he'll hurt her, at least until he gets what he wants," Soo announces, his voice calm and even.

I advance on him. "And what if hurting her is what he wants? He's just as much a monster as I am. As you are," I spit. "What stops him from putting a bullet in her head? He has no control. All it takes is her saying one stupid thing."

A chill settles over my shoulders. What if she's already dead, and I don't get to—? No, I can't even consider it. Or a lot of people are going to die tonight, starting with Lucas.

With Soo out of the way, I stalk to the motorcycle, sitting in the corner of the garage, and kick it hard enough to knock it over. It scrapes against the concrete, and Soo lets out a huff behind me. He's always loved Lucas's motorcycle, and this one is my brother's pride and joy. I can't get to him at this moment. I can't rip his fucking head off his body, so I'll take it out on the closest thing he loves, this fucking bike.

I stomp on the custom lever seat, bending the metal, warping it as it bounces between my shoe and the concrete.

Since it's metal, there is nothing else I can do to it, but I enjoy staring down at the warped metal. Even if it's not ruined, he'll have to do some work to make it rideable again. If he's alive once I'm done with him.

Soo clears his throat. "You good man?"

I spin and glare. "Do I look fucking good? I'm about five seconds from finding the nearest loaded weapon and stalking the streets until I find her."

Instead of arguing, Soo holds his hands up in surrender. "I get it. You want to find her. You're worried about her. Like I said, I don't think Lucas will hurt her. I think more than anything, more than revenge even, he wants answers."

"Answers to what?" I stare down at the addresses again and stalk to the nearest SUV. Soo climbs into the driver's side, of course. It's his own way to exert control in our partnership, plus he fears for his life when I drive.

"Your brother is a walking fucking question mark. Your opposite. Where you're resolved, he's unsettled. You made yourself a Diavolo when you lost family. He's still that little boy watching his mother be slaughtered and needing to know why. It's not Celia he wants; it's her father."

He pulls away, no doubt having already memorized each location on the list. I ignore his comment about Lucas because it's something I already know. And Lucas's disquiet has always felt like a failure on my part.

But as we make it to the garage gate, his phone chimes. He answers, and I stare at him impatiently, waiting to find out what information he's found.

"It's one of my sources. He thinks he saw your brother buying food in one of the areas he sells his product."

Something surges in my chest, demanding freedom. "Where?"

"A Chinese restaurant. It's not near any of the addresses on the list. Let's head there and see if we can get more information. If he orders delivery to where he stays over there, then the restaurant might have the information on file."

He pulls away, and I squeeze the handle above the door to keep myself from venting my rage on the vehicle. When we get to my brother, it will not be good. Especially if he hurt her.

She better not have a single mark on her pale skin. Or I'm going to—

I shake off the violent thoughts trying to force their way into my mind. Think rationally. He won't be unprotected in his safe house, and I'm in no condition for strategic planning.

As if he can read my mind, Soo says, "What's the plan when we get there? Maybe you should let me talk, so we don't end up having to buy a Chinese restaurant to cover anything up."

I glare, even though his eyes are fixed out the windshield. "Not in the mood for jokes."

"Who's joking?"

I release my death grip on the handle and rub my face. It's sometime in the morning, and I glance at the clock. Four a.m. "Is this restaurant even open right now?"

"Twenty-four hours, according to my source, but he's not sure if the same workers are on duty that saw Lucas."

Instead of engaging my asshat friend further, I stare out the window into the dead city streets. I've always liked this time of morning, but now, I can't grasp the calm it usually brings me. Not with my gut roiling, and my brain running over everything Lucas could have done to her in the hours he's held her captive.

We stop outside a tiny hole-in-the-wall restaurant with neon lights on the window. Soo climbs out, and I follow, but he slams the door in my face. With a growl, I yank it open and stand on the threshold, waiting.

He doesn't see me lingering, and that's fine because the moment he learns what I need to know, I'm leaving his ass here and finding my brother on my own. Even if I have to tear apart this entire street to do it.

While Soo is waiting for the manager to come out of the kitchen, I glance up and down the block. It's not upscale, but it's not exactly low-end either. There are a couple of new high-rises on the corner, and I'd bet good money Lucas is in one of them. He may like to play the bad boy, but the man is a sucker for his creature comforts.

Soo's voice drifts from the restaurant, and I tilt my head to focus on what the little old lady is saying. And it sounds an awful lot like she is saying she can't give Soo the information he wants.

I step into the shop, ready and willing to extract what I need. Hurting a grandma isn't at the top of my favorite things list, but it doesn't mean, for Celia's sake, I won't do what is necessary.

Soo raises his voice so I can hear. "He's my friend. He won't hurt you, but he can pay you. Name a price, and the money is yours."

And this is exactly why he handles our logistics. My brain always goes straight to violence. Soo prefers gentle negotiation before resorting to using his fists. Even if no one can stand against him once he gets to that point.

The woman rattles off an address, and I shove out the glass door and onto the street, already taking in the road signs.

"Hey, man, got something for me," a homeless man says from behind a cardboard box.

I stare down at him and then back at the shop, where Soo hasn't even noticed I left. The man doesn't move as I dig through my pocket and pull out a hundred-dollar bill. Crouching, careful not to touch him, I extend the money.

"This isn't a freebie. It's for a job."

"What do you want," he grates out, his words sloppy.

"A man is about to walk out of this shop. When he looks around, tell him calmly that you saw a big guy run off down the street, in the opposite direction I'm about to walk. Can you do that?"

"Yep, I can."

I nod and release the money to his dirty fingers. There's no telling if he'll do as he's told, but at the very least, he might buy me a few minutes from Soo.

I walk down the sidewalk quickly, glancing over my shoulder, but Soo hasn't come back out yet. Good. My brother and I are about to have a conversation, and I want to have it alone.

If it ends with a bullet in his brain, so be it. Soo can see Lucas when he comes to clean up the mess.

A buzz fills my ears as I reach the building. It has a keypad entry and locked doors. Not that it matters. I pull out a knife I keep in my pocket with a glass break nodule at the end of the handle and press it into the pristine glass.

Lucas better hope he doesn't have a doorman, or this night is going to get messier and messier.

I unlock the heavy door, enter, and head straight to the elevator. As the door closes, I'm alone, and the shiny steel doors reflect my unhinged smile.

I made the mistake of thinking I could live without her before, but I won't make that mistake twice. Celia is mine, and no one will stand in my way. Least of all, my little fucking brother.

4

CELIA

I'm tired. So fucking tired. I lay my head on my arms as I sit at Lucas's countertop. It's not just that I want to burrow into bed and sleep for a hundred years. It's a bone-deep exhaustion radiating out, sinking into my heart and mind. Will I ever be able to shake it?

Lucas snaps his fingers in front of my face a couple of times, and I jerk away from them. "What? What do you want? Can you just let me sleep for a little while, and I'll tell you anything you want to know?"

He narrows his eyes at me until my own droop heavily and obscure him into a blurry man shape on the other side of the countertop. "No, we are going to finish this now. I don't know how much time I have, and I plan to get everything I need out of you before it's up."

My head snaps up at that little revelation. "What do you mean, you don't know how much time you have? Are you going to kill me?" I hate the desperate edge to my tone. Even though I don't want to die, I won't beg him. At least not yet.

He doesn't answer my question, of course. "Don't worry about that. All you need to worry about right now is telling me what I want to know. So, I repeat, how many people live and work in your father's house?"

My brain is fuzzy from sleep and, no doubt, trauma. "I don't know. My father, my mother..." I swallow the words about my sister. No, she doesn't live there anymore. "The chef, there are several maids, drivers, security. I can't know how many people my father employs when I only interact with a handful of them. Not to mention what might have changed in the weeks your brother held me captive."

"Where does your father go when he leaves the house?"

I gape at him and the randomness of the question. "How the hell should I know? It's not like he tells me his daily routine. Mostly he stays at home and works out of his office. There's a cabin he goes to every so often to fish or whatever men do in the woods, but otherwise," I say again, "I don't know."

Lucas leans over the counter, pinning me under his glare. "You better start thinking fast, or this is going to get a lot more physical."

While Lucas is scary, he's not Nicolo. No one can match the raw intensity his brother exudes, and having been on the receiving end several times, Lucas just isn't cutting it. "I understand you want answers, but I can't tell you something I don't know. And threatening me into what, making shit up? How is that going to help either of us?"

He goes from stillness to motion as fast as Nicolo does, sending a glass against his kitchen wall in one smooth swat. It shatters, and I duck my face to ensure none of the shards reach me. Where Nicolo is in control, Lucas is an F-5 tornado headed for a city. As I expected, he's not finished. He stalks around the counter and drags my stool to face him. My entire body shudders beneath his dark eyes.

"Where are the guards housed on your property?"

It's a simple question, one I actually know the answer to, and yet, I still want to lie and throw it back in his face. But I don't. The faster he ends this, the faster he might release me. "They are mostly housed in the underground garage. There's a sort of barracks down there, and the security team lives and works out of it."

If he's happy I can finally answer something, he doesn't show it. Oh. It was a test. He's throwing in control questions to see if I'm lying.

He grips the stool, and I lift my chin, determined not to cower to him.

"And where do your parents sleep in the house?"

It's cute how he thinks my parents share a living space. "My father is on the ground floor near his study. My mother sleeps on the third floor near her library. Why does that matter? You'll have a shit time getting through security to reach them."

He leans in to growl in my face. "No one had trouble getting in to retrieve you, did they?"

I still and consider this. No, but they got help from fucking Marco to get me out of there. However, someone in security should have noticed the goons who carried me out of the house. The image of the dead men's blood all over Nicolo floats to the surface of my mind, but I shove it back down. Now is not the time to let my emotional trauma take over.

"Did you help kidnap me that first time?" I counter with a question.

He shoves away from me and heads back into the kitchen to gulp down some water. On the outside, he might look calmer, but he's pacing back and forth, running his hands through his already mussed hair. He's a caged, starved lion, and I'm the dangling steak.

"No, I didn't help, but I would have if Nic asked me to. I would have kidnapped you and gotten my revenge that first night."

Something in me snaps, and I jump off the stool and launch myself at him. I'm done being the docile woman, being kidnapped, and tossed around. "I'm not some fucking Barbie doll to be snatched out of her house and passed around to everyone who god damn thinks I have some kind of value!" I scream, and without thinking, I pound my fists into his very firm chest.

I don't get far with my assault. His huge hands grip onto my wrists, and he drags my arms back down to my sides, leaning into my face with a vindictive smile on his lips.

"You do that again, and you'll regret it. Just because we're blood-related doesn't mean I care about you. I won't think twice about hurting you."

"Then hurt me because I have no information for you."

He blows out a breath and shakes his head. "Why are you protecting him when you already know how much of a monster he is?"

I shake in his hold, trying to pry myself loose. "I'm not protecting him. I'm protecting myself."

Lucas snaps, his features darken, and the fine hairs on the back of my neck stand on end. "Stop fucking lying to me!" he roars, shaking me until my head lolls around. "You know he killed your sister, right? Our fucking sister. She's dead, Celia, because she didn't want to marry the man he decided she should. He would have done the same to you."

My chest seizes up, refusing to gather air, refusing to let me speak.

His grip loosens, and his hands fall away from my skin. "He shot her in the fucking head himself and then told everyone she committed suicide."

All the pain from my sister's death comes rushing back. It's like trying to breathe around a balloon as I hear my mother's voice growling at me to keep my chin up and stop blubbering. I see the pale, cold skin of my sister's eyelids closed forever. I taste the salt of my tears, which never seem to stop rolling down my cheeks.

Her loss punched a hole in my heart. My best friend is gone, and there is no way to bring her back. I don't think about what I'm doing. I simply react. Dragging my hand up, I slap him hard across the face. His head jerks to the side as a wash of pain flares up my fingers and into my arm.

"What is wrong with you? Why would you say something so disgusting?"

Before I can fully grasp what is happening, another kind of pain hits me as his hand contacts my cheek. He hits me with an open palm, the sharp smack burning across my cheek. I can't really say I'm surprised. Lucas isn't the type of man you can hurt without hurting you back to the same degree. It should hurt more, but compared to the ache now taking root in my chest, nothing can hurt like that.

"Hit me again, and I'll make sure it's the last time."

The pain means nothing to me, and I grit my teeth as I speak, "Then shut your fucking mouth about my sister. *My* sister. You didn't even know her, so don't talk about her."

He cocks his head to the side. "Is that the problem, Celia? You fear our relationship because if we share the same blood, maybe you're a little more like me than you want to be? Maybe you have what it takes to make your father pay for what he took from you."

I swallow against a wave of bile forcing its way up my throat and stare at the floor. It's not that I fear I'm like Lucas. He's more like his insane-ass brother than me. It's that I fear what I'm going to do to my father the next time I see him, if what Lucas told me is true. And yet, even as I want to doubt every single word, I know in my heart he's not lying. What does he have to lie to me for?

He shoves past me, causing me to stumble into the side of the counter. I use the cold countertop to steady myself and get a grip. If I don't remain calm, I won't be able to get out of here. That is, if he doesn't ultimately plan to kill me.

I keep him in the corner of my eye as I walk back around to the stool and sit. He crosses the room and strips out of his shirt, then drags a heavy punching bag on a chain from the corner of the room.

"If you're going to workout, then let me sleep."

He delivers a solid punch to the grey vinyl, making it swing on its hook. "No, the only reason I'm doing this right now is so I don't vent my frustration out on your face. Be grateful and start thinking of things I might want to know about your father."

When he turns back to the bag, he starts up a furious pace against it. As each punch echoes through the room, I flinch, thinking about him hitting me with those powerful fists. With his shirt off and in actual lighting, I can see more of his skin. His scarred and bruised skin. Almost from the edge of his pants all the way up his shoulders are bruises in various stages of healing, old scars and nicks breaking up the purple splotches.

"What the hell happened to you?" I ask, knowing I shouldn't engage him. I should let him think I want to help him in whatever stupid thing he's got planned.

Of course, he doesn't deign to answer me, so I get up and cross the room to look at him better. Yes, all along his ribs are large rings of purple. Like someone took a baseball bat to his midsection. "Did Nicolo do that to you? You didn't let him, right? Why would he hurt you like that?"

Even knowing what little I do about his brother, I can't see him beating Lucas for no apparent reason. Not unless he did something that angered him. Nicolo punished me on every occasion he could think about, but usually never without a warning.

I move closer, standing a few feet from his elbow. "You should wrap those up and maybe ice them. They look painful."

"I'm fine," he grits out. "I like to fight on the weekend. You know, let loose. Some people go dancing, I'll smash in someone's skull. Same thing."

I'm not surprised by his words, but I am surprised that he is sharing something about himself with me, no matter how cruel it is.

"Go sit down, or our little break from questioning is going to be over, and I promise, the next round will be far more physical."

I wave at his body. "But it looks like you're in pain. You could have broken ribs; you should see a doctor and get yourself checked out."

He steadies the bag as it swings away and faces me. "I don't need to see a doctor, and I don't care if it hurts. The pain reminds me I'm alive. I want the pain. Now, go sit the fuck down and get out of my face."

I blink at the bite in his voice and the rage in his tone. He likes the pain? What is he, a sadist? It's obvious he's not used to people looking at him, caring for him, noticing him even, not in the shadow of his brother. That strikes something within me. I'd always been the little sister, the less pretty, less tall, less everything version of my sister.

Hoping to get through to him, I touch his shoulder softly, gentling my tone. "You deserve to take care of yourself. Remaining in pain won't change anything."

His fingers tighten around the bag in front of him. "What would you know about it, princess?" I flinch at the pet name for me. He definitely doesn't call me princess like Nicolo does. His tone is all murderous rage. "You were pampered and spoiled, brought up in your mansion with anything and everything you wanted. After our parents died, we had to scrape and claw our way to the top. And every day, we have to fight to stay here. So, don't give me any of your bullshit. You don't know what it's like to starve, to sleep on the streets. To wonder if the last breath you took will be the final one."

He shoves the bag back into the corner and slips his shirt back over his head. "Since you seem to want to talk, let's return to my questions."

I retreat a few steps, but he doesn't let me get far, grasping my upper arm to drag me toward him. "Does your father have any fears?"

"If he does, he never told me them," I whisper, trying to rectify this man in front of me with every version he presents. The man who saved me from the auction block to this fearsome fighter in front of me.

"Are you sure about that?" he asks, tightening his grip.

A bolt of pain lights up my arm. I want to be strong, to be fierce, but there is no fighting with Lucas. "You're hurting me. Let go."

"Answer the question."

"I'm fucking sure he's never mentioned any fears to me. We've never been a sharing sort of family, and even if we were, no one confesses their fears out loud."

Instead of releasing me, he tightens his hold. Pins and needles shoot down my limb in time with my racing heart.

"Fine. No fears that you know of, but joys? How about those? Anything he loves most since obviously, you and your sister aren't on that list."

My mouth drops open. He's an asshole. "Is that necessary? Why are you doing this? I understand you want answers, fine, but you don't need to hurt me, and you don't need to be a dick."

Lucas cocks his head. "Are you this mouthy with my brother?"

"Yes, and he punishes me for it every single time."

His eyes narrow, and his mouth tips up at one side. "Oh, I've heard how he likes to punish you."

My face flames hot, and I glance away. If he wants to hurt me, at the very least, I won't give him the satisfaction of seeing it in my eyes. "Besides his cigar collection, I don't know of anything my father loves. Well, outside of power. He enjoys being in charge of any situation he finds himself in. If he's not, then he won't do it."

He gives me a little shake, a new slice of pain radiating down to my fingers. "Is that all you have?

"Fuck, yes. Now, let me go." I try to pull my arm from his grasp, but once he lets me go, his other hand clamps around my neck as he slowly backs me toward the wall.

"I'm done playing games. The only reason I saved your worthless life was to find out the worst possible way to murder your father, but if you can't tell me that, then you're useless to me, and I might as well kill you."

I clamp my mouth shut and stare at him. If he wants me to beg, he's going to have to work a lot harder than that.

"Nothing? Well…" He pulls a knife from his pants and flicks it open smoothly. But he doesn't do more than hover the pointed tip near my cheek.

It's a line in the sand. Which one of us will break first? Because I can see in his eyes, he won't kill me. At the very least, to protect himself from his brother's rage.

Maybe he can tell what I'm thinking because he says, "I don't have to kill you to make you hurt. Or give you a matching scar on your other cheek."

And yet, he only stares into my eyes as if daring me to make him cut me.

"You won't." I shake my head slightly, careful not to touch the blade.

"Why wouldn't I? You mean nothing to me."

"Because you're not like him." I don't have to explain that I'm talking about our father. Something in Lucas's eyes changes. Surprise, maybe? Realization?

Before I can say more, the door bursts inward, slamming against the dining room wall. On the threshold is Nicolo, his gaze promising murder, his eyes fixed on Lucas.

*T*he eye of a hurricane is a trick. There's nothing quiet or calm about it. The eye is there for the target to realize the storm has only just begun.

And this calm settling over me as I survey the scene in my brother's safe house is nothing more than a warning. Too bad he won't be able to do anything about it.

I carefully shut the front door behind me and stalk forward. Lucas turns to put his back against the wall and pulls Celia tight into his chest; the glint of a knife shines in the light as he brings it to her throat. I know my brother well enough to know if he wanted to kill her, she would already be dead. This isn't about wanting to hurt her. It's about trying to save his own ass. And I suspect, more of a reaction than a threat.

Instead of focusing my attention on him, I survey her, cataloging the leggings she has on and the oversized T-shirt she's wearing. The shirt is one of his own, and I want to rip it off her body. My eyes roam her beautiful face, even with her makeup half crusted on her face, I've never seen a more beautiful woman.

There's a red mark on her cheek, and I step forward to rub my thumb over it. Her big brown eyes are wide, staring up at me, awaiting my reaction.

"Did he hurt you, princess?"

"Why? You didn't care if I was going to get hurt when you sold me." She throws the words into my face, and I force myself not to react.

"Tell me," I order. "If you don't, I'll assume he did."

She shakes her head frantically. "No, he didn't hurt me."

Now that she's confirmed as unharmed, I lift my gaze to my brother and let all that boiling rage spill over the surface.

Knowing my next move, and no doubt feeling the change in the air, he shoves Celia away, and she stumbles behind me. At least he has the presence of mind to get her out of the way before I beat the shit out of him. It's enough to keep me from killing him. For now.

I don't have time to see if she's okay before Lucas comes swinging at me with the knife still tucked into his fist.

"You'd stab me, brother? After everything we've been through." I blink, shutting down my feelings, my thought process.

He huffs as I pry the knife from his grip and throw it across the room. "You're going to do a lot worse to me. I can see it in your eyes."

I punch him in the stomach, causing him to double over while I use my other hand and grip him by the back of his neck. "You are so right. But the difference is, you deserve it. You stole something that belongs to me, and I'm here to get it back. As my brother, you should've known better, but it seems you don't care. Therefore, I won't care what happens to you while you suffer the consequences of your actions."

Celia steps into the corner of my vision, and I meet her gaze. "Please, don't hurt him. You'll end up killing him if you keep hitting him like that."

"Shut the fuck up," Lucas yells at her while scrambling to get out of my hold. He thinks I'm distracted by her presence, but I'm hyperfocused on protecting her.

I lift him by his neck and slam him into the wall. Then deliver several more blows, one to his face and two to the ribcage. He grunts and slides to the floor in a heap. My knuckles are split from the force of my punches, and my hand throbs, but the pain doesn't matter to me. I thrive on it. It's like a drug. Each blow I deliver is another hit of dopamine to the brain.

"Please, stop!" Celia screeches from behind me. But I can't stop, not now that I can finally let all the festering rage out.

I drag him back up by the hair and pull his face to mine. I grit my teeth as I speak. "Did you fuck her? Is that why you wanted her? You wanted a taste of her so badly you had to steal her away to get it?"

Celia gasps from behind me, but my gaze never wavers. The look in Lucas's eyes is one I understand all too well. It's self-loathing, hate, and rage swirling into a tornado that will only end up destroying him.

"No, I didn't touch her like that," he spits through blood-stained teeth.

I nod, and there is a slight ease of rage that uncoils from within my gut. "And that's the only reason I will not kill you right now."

I hit him again, enjoying the way the pain rips through my arm and my shoulder as it makes contact with his body.

"Please," Celia whispers behind me. An ache builds in my chest as I turn to look at her. In all the times I held her, she'd never begged me like that, never for herself. But she will for him? For another fucking man?

I release my grip and he slides to the floor. I let him stay there, his head lolling side to side as he grapples with consciousness.

She's on her knees, tears ringing her beautiful eyes, and I crouch in front of her so I can look at her better. "Why? Why are you begging for his life when he kidnapped you again? Why beg for his life when you didn't even beg me for your own?"

Without blinking, she says, "He saved me. If it weren't for him, I would be a sex slave right now."

Her words deliver another blow. She doesn't know I was coming back for her, and I doubt she'd believe me if I told her. I sold her, and I can never take that back. Still, I don't think that's the only reason. There is more, something she isn't telling me.

I shake my head and lift her chin, forcing our gazes together. "Not good enough. Tell me why you really want to save him. Give me a reason I'll actually buy."

Her shuddering exhale tells me more than she thinks. "Lucas is my half-brother."

"Excuse me?" I'm taken aback by her response.

"Lucas is my half-brother, but before you freak out, we are not related." She waves a hand at him before her arm falls limply back to her sides. "He saved me because he thinks I can tell him about my father, our father, but I want answers too, and if you kill him, then neither of us will get those."

I shrug. "What does that matter to me?"

Her shoulders slump back as tears slip from her eyes and down the apples of her cheeks. My gaze gravitates to the red mark on her pale skin, and the pulsing need to pummel Lucas all over again reappears.

"Maybe I don't want you to lose your only brother? I don't want you to kill him, least of all for me. There's no going back from that. I won't be the cause for his blood on your hands."

"You've called me a monster more times than I can count. What makes you think I give a shit? You're mine, Celia. He knew that, and still, he took you from me. So, I'll ask you one more time, princess, and you need to give me a straight answer, one worthy of his life. Why is it so important to you he stays alive?"

This time she doesn't have an answer for me, and I'm through being patient. I stand and tower over her. "Well, if you don't have a good enough reason, then give me a moment. I'll take care of him, and then we can leave this place for good."

She grabs my fist between her smaller palms, trying to stop me. "Please. He's my brother too." The words come out deflated. "I already lost my sister, and even if he's fucking crazy, I can't lose my only real family."

Her brother. She *did* really say that a moment ago—the words *real family* ring inside my head.

I pause, and while my mind wants to fall into the implications of that statement, I can't, not while she's touching me of her own volition. Not while she's wearing another fucking man's clothes, not while she's in someone else's house.

I tug her hand off mine and throw it away. "I still don't care who the fuck he is to you. You are mine."

Still on her knees, she turns and tries to scramble away from me when she catches the look in my eyes. But there is no time. I reach down, snag her ankle and come down on my knees hard around her thighs.

Then I turn her onto her back and press her under my weight to the floor, so our faces line up, and she can't possibly escape. "You're mine." I grit through my teeth. Even knowing how fucked up and wrong it is, I can't possibly envision ever letting her go.

Her voice is pitiful when she finally answers. "I don't belong to anyone but myself."

I gently scoop stray bits of her hair off her tear-streaked face and smile. "Oh no, princess, you were mine from the moment I brought you home. I was just too stubborn to realize it."

"Last night, you sold me to some old man. You didn't care about me then. I wasn't *yours* then. What could have changed since last night? I won't go with you only to be re-sold to someone worse."

I grind into her, relearning how the curves of her body fit to mine, my cock already growing hard, despite the urge to set this place on fire with my bastard brother inside it.

"No. You belong to me, and only to me, from this day forward. I was wrong to think I could give you up. Wrong to think that this was merely revenge. No one else will look at you." I trace the swell of her breasts under the T-shirt, which is pulled tight between us. "No one else will touch you." She wriggles underneath me as I map the pretty little cupid's bow of her full lips with my fingers. "No one else will even so much as say your name, or I'll kill them and fuck you in a puddle of their blood just to prove how much you're mine."

Her chest presses up against me, even as she tries to wiggle out of my hold. "Why are you doing this? Just let me go home, please."

"I'll take you home, *stellina*. To our home."

Celia snarls her pretty lips. "You know that's not what I mean. I want to go to my own home. I want to get as far away from both of you assholes as I can get."

I draw my nose up the column of her neck, breathing her in. Despite her activities, a faint floral aroma clings to her skin. I want to taste her, rip her clothes off and rub against her, to imprint my scent on her. I want to mark her, so everyone knows she belongs to me and only me. "Stop squirming. I'm two seconds away from ripping your clothes off because he gave them to you. Another man put them on you, brother or not."

She shoves at my chest, as if her meager attempts at freedom will dislodge me. "He didn't help me put them on. I got dressed all on my own, like a big girl," she mocks.

Any other day, and I might punish her for giving me such sass, but right now, all I can think about is her body under mine and how good it will feel when I sink inside her wet heat. I'll be her first and last. She continues struggling against me, and every little squirm makes my cock grow harder. I don't bother hiding it. Instead, I grind against her core, using her to bring me back from the brink of anger.

"Mmm, you feel so good, *stellina*. Even better than I remember," I whisper into the shell of her ear.

Again, she tries to shove me off, but this time, I capture her wrists and pin them to the floor near her head.

Lucas moans behind me. The stubborn fucker is trying to get up. He won't be getting off this floor until I walk out the door with Celia in my arms. Not if I have anything to say about it.

Celia draws my attention back to her as she bucks her hips up to get free, and I only chuckle against her mouth. "Oh, I wouldn't do that if you want to walk out of here with your clothes on. I told you, I'm seconds away from ripping every stitch from your body. Don't tempt me because we both know I would do it."

"Fuck you," she growls into my face as she slips from my grasp.

I don't let her get away. I chase her back to the floor and capture her lips against mine. Taking her mouth in a hard kiss, I slip my tongue against the seam of her mouth, and even as angry as she is with me, a flame of fire burning in my hands, she opens to me.

She nips at my tongue, her brown eyes blazing, and I lift my head to glare down at her. "Bite me again, and we'll be playing a different game, princess, and surely one you will not win."

When she settles her head back to the floor, I lean in and run my lips over hers gently. This time she remains still, refusing to acknowledge me. It's hard to play the ice queen when I can feel the heat of her body through the thin leggings she's wearing.

"I hate you," she sneers.

I slam her hands together above her head, so I can hold both in one of mine. Then I pinch her chin in my hold and search her face. "You don't hate me, and lying about it won't help your situation. You hate how much you want me and how much I remind you of it."

"I do hate you," she says, this time, screaming it inches from my face.

With a shove, I pin her to the floor by her chin and stare down into her eyes. I don't know what she sees there, but she stops fighting long enough for me to speak again. "I don't give a shit if you hate me. I don't give a shit if you want to kill me. Hell, I don't even give a shit if you try to run every chance you get, but know this, you belong to me, and nothing you or anyone else says or does will change that. From now on, if anyone so much as breathes in your general direction, I will fucking gut them. Nod if you understand."

Instead of giving in and bending to my will, she narrows her eyes and spits in my face.

I let out a long-shuddering exhale and wipe my face across the front of her shirt. When I look at her again, a smile tugs at my lips.

"You want your juices on me, princess? All you had to do was ask."

I reach between us and grip her cunt hard in my palm. A squeak escapes her, and I revel in the sound as I flex my fingers against her warm, pants-covered pussy. I don't let her get off that easily. I press my face into her neck, trailing my nose up and down her throat, stopping just below her ear. For a second, I pause, and a soft exhale passes her lips. I smile against her skin before I sink my teeth into the flesh there and listen joyfully as a cry of pain fills the air. When she struggles, I bite harder, and the need to mark every single inch of her body festers in my mind.

When I lift my mouth from her neck, I see a pink circle from where my teeth were indented in her skin.

"I'd tattoo my name across every inch of you if I could," I whisper against the bite mark. "And I told you, I bite harder."

I need to be inside her, in every hole, forcing her to take my cock until we're both spent. I want my scent on her skin, and my cum rubbed into her creamy thighs. My cock is hard as a rock as I lift off her and drag her to her feet.

Immediately, she fights, but I grab her by the throat and pull her in to meet my eyes. "Walk out of this building like a normal person, or I'll carry you over my shoulder. It's your choice, there are no other options. I won't fight you all the way to the lobby."

"You can't do this," she whispers. The look in her eyes tells me exactly how she's feeling, how broken and sad she is. I can't pay attention to that right now. Not when we're still here in this apartment, and she is still wearing my brother's clothes.

Speaking of brothers, I stare down at Lucas, still writhing on the floor. When I punched him, I didn't think I'd hit him that hard. Oh well, he'll learn his lesson over the next few days while he is questioned.

My phone has been buzzing since I got here, and when I dig it out to check, there are several messages from Soo. I don't respond to his demands but order him to get a guy up here to drag my brother home.

Once that's taken care of, I turn my attention back to Celia. "Let's go, princess. Before I strip you down and take you on that countertop. I'm fucking starved for you."

Her mouth drops open, but she shakes it off quickly. "Is that all I'm going to be to you, a warm place you can park your dick? A sex doll?"

I grip the back of her neck and maneuver her around the furniture and out to the hallway. "I suspect, if you were a sex doll, you'd be putting up significantly less fight, and you'd be a lot more fucking quiet."

My rage has cooled, but the need I feel for her is only just starting its consuming path through me. The urge to mark her, claim her, ensure any man who looks at her knows who she belongs to is maddening. For Celia, I feel primal.

I shove her down the hallway and maintain my grip on her neck. She stumbles over her feet, but I keep her standing upright, pressing her forward until we reach the elevator. It's a quick ride down to the bottom floor, and by Soo's texts, I know he already has the car waiting outside.

We walk out the building, and Celia shivers. I'd offer her my jacket, but in a few moments, she won't need it since I'll be warming her up from the inside out.

As we approach the car, Soo exits the driver's side and opens the door for me so I don't have to release my grip on her. With a gentle shove, I force Celia inside the car. She scrambles across the leather and immediately tries to open the opposite door, but it's already locked.

Turning in her seat, she stares at me with disdain. All I can do is smile.

"Now, princess, you didn't think it would be that easy, did you?"

6

CELIA

*T*he leather seats creak as I slide around to put my back against the door since it won't open. I turn to face him. I can't fight him off; he's proven that fact to me more times than I care to remember. There is never a time when I'm not reminded that Nic is the predator and I am the prey.

As he settles into the other seat, I can feel him vibrating with violence. I didn't make it easy on myself, fighting him back there, and I'm sure he's about to make me regret it.

Everything he said is spinning through my head to the cadence of you're mine, you're mine, you're mine. He declared it like he made the choice for both of us, all but telling me I'll never be free of him.

I watch the door through the window as we idle at the curb, and Soo comes out lugging Lucas between him and another of Nicolo's men.

Nicolo pinches my chin between two fingers and drags my gaze away from them. "He's alive. You don't need to worry about him. Right now, you need to worry about yourself."

I swallow hard, my heart trying to punch into my throat. "What are you going to do with me now?"

A wicked smile curls his lips as he drops his gaze down my body. "Anything and everything I want. You're mine, after all."

His words shouldn't ignite a fire in me. They should leave me cold and terrified, and I guess part of me is terrified. But the memory of how he can make my body feel is drilling through that fear, making it harder for me to see. The pleasure he's given me, even through the humiliation and pain, is all there, tucked away like a secret. I've yet to examine how I feel about it all as I'd gotten stuck on the whole selling me part of our relationship. And with the way he's staring at me, now isn't the time to dissect it either.

One thing I am certain of is that I have to forget the pleasure he brought me and remember that he's the villain here—because if I slip up and fall into his web, I'll be as good as dead.

"What about what I want?"

He snaps his hand out and drags me to him by the throat. His grip is firm but gentle, with no pressure, more like persuasive positioning. "What you want right now is irrelevant. And will be until I erase every other man from your life, starting with Lucas."

I brace for whatever he's about to do to me, but I'm not prepared for him to rip my T-shirt clean down the center. Cool air meets my heated skin, making my nipples hard. I immediately look around in a panic. Nic's driver is just pulling the car away. The windows are tinted anyway, but there is no partition between the front and the back seat, meaning that the guy behind the wheel can very much hear us.

"Take off your pants and underwear, or I'll rip them off too."

Before he can repeat himself, I'm shucking the ripped edges of my shirt from my arms and moving to the waistband of my leggings.

"What am I going to wear, then? Do you want everyone to see me naked?"

I glance to the front seat, where his driver has his eyes trained to the road.

"Don't worry about him." He unbuttons his shirt, tugs it off, and lays it over the back of the seat beside him. "For after," he explains.

After what?

I can't control my heavy breathing as I lift my hips and toss away the pants and underwear. My hands are trembling, so I tuck them between my knees. So he doesn't see how nervous I am. At least, it makes me feel better to think he doesn't see. Of course, he notices everything, and he won't let me hide.

He drags my hands to his thigh and sits them there while he unbuckles his slacks and shoves them down, his rock-hard cock springing free.

I suck in a breath and jerk my hand back, but he captures it again and brings it to his skin. "Rub me," he orders.

Okay, this isn't so bad. If all he wants is a hand job, maybe he and I can manage this negotiation. I grip him tight, and he wraps his hand around mine. "I won't last long, but I need to come, and I'm going to mark you with it. Rub it into your skin, so you smell like me and feel me all over your body."

A heavy throb starts in my clit, but I don't dare shift for fear he'll see it and know.

He doesn't release my hand and drops his head against the seat as he thrusts into both of our grips. It only takes a few minutes for his thighs to tighten up, his breathing to quicken, and his other hand to reach out and latch onto my upper thigh.

God, he looks so beautiful like this. I hate him for it even while I'm throbbing as I watch him.

"Fuck, you have no idea how much I want to be inside you right now. Slamming deep inside your tight pussy, claiming you over and over again. I'll be your first and last, Celia. Your virgin blood will coat my cock, and there will never be another man who gets the pleasure of touching you." If only his words were true and something I could believe.

With a few more strokes, he comes hard, his warm seed splashes all over our hands, and then he locks eyes with me as he takes the cum and rubs it into my breasts. Keeping his eyes trained on me, he watches with intent until the last of the hot liquid is caked into my skin.

I'm sticky with it, and the smell of him permeates the air around us. As he wipes his hand on his pants, I risk squeezing my thighs together to relieve some of the ache there.

I convince myself if this is all he wants from me, a hand job and to sit next to him naked, I can deal with it. I can handle it.

It doesn't take long for me to realize how naïve and stupid I am.

He reaches across the car and drags me into his side. "That was just a little taste, *stellina*. I need so much more of you. All of you. By the time I'm finished with you, you will be mine in every way possible."

I shudder in his grip and shake my head. "Is this how it's going to be? You, using me to get off, but never even bothering to ask what I want?" I shouldn't be surprised that nothing between us has changed.

I catch the way he drops his gaze down to my breasts, even in the darkness of the back seat. "I don't have to ask. I know what you need. You don't think I can see how much you want me? I bet if I lay you down on this seat, you'll be soaking my balls in seconds. Tell me I'm wrong."

When I don't answer, an urgency fills his touch. He captures my head between his hands and lowers me to his lap, his cock already hard against his belly again. "Suck it and suck it good because you want to get it nice and wet. Afterward, I'm fucking your ass, and how soaked I am will determine how comfortable it will be for you."

Before I can call him a bastard, he forces my mouth onto his dick. I suck in a breath through my nose, already tasting the salty musk of his cum and his skin. The longer I take to do this, the longer he will hold me down and force me. Tears are already building at the corners of my eyes as I add my hand into the mix so he doesn't gag me on his length.

Once I take over on my own volition, he lessens his hold on my head and gently twines his fingers into my hair. "Harder, *stellina*. Or I'll do it myself, and with the way I feel right now, I won't be gentle with you."

I focus on my task, squeezing my eyes closed, tears streaking down my cheeks.

His hand trails from my hair over the curve of my naked spine down to my ass. Then he delves his fingers between my legs, gently inserting two digits into my pussy.

I gasp against him, inadvertently taking him deeper into my mouth.

"That's it," he growls.

With his fingers inside me, I can't focus. My technique is sloppy, my hands jerky as I work them from his base to my mouth with each pass. His thighs tremble underneath my braced forearms, and I squeeze myself around his fingers, needing more.

"My princess is greedy for it. I'll give it to you soon, don't worry. Faster," he whispers, urging me on.

When I don't increase my pace, he arches his hips up into my face. It pushes me off balance, and I almost topple off the seat. I sit up and glare. But he's too far gone to care. He catches me around the neck and rolls me onto my back, staring down at me.

His fingers circle my throat, squeezing, but not enough to cut off air. "When I tell you to do something, you'll do it. Even if you don't want to do it. Even if it goes against every single thing you believe in. You'll do it, and you'll act like you enjoy it."

The heat I felt before sparks into anger, and I glare back at him. "Is that what you want? A woman who pretends to like your cock? I'd think you wouldn't have trouble finding a willing woman; why keep one who doesn't want you?"

Ruthlessly, he spears me with two fingers, sinking deep. The air in my lungs evaporates. The pleasure he is giving me hinges on pain, but I wouldn't stop him, couldn't even if I tried.

"You can lie all you want, but your body will always betray you. It would take me two minutes to make you come around my fingers right now. The only problem is I don't reward brats who can't follow simple directions."

Before I can respond, he flips me onto my belly and drags my hips up to meet his.

"I warned you, and you wanted to fight about it. Now I'm going to take you as is, and it's not going to be as good for you as it could've been."

I whimper and try to drag my hips away, to crawl to the door and claw at the handle to get out.

He stops my advance and wraps his arm around my waist, pressing himself against my ass, and with the other hand, he rubs his cock between my pussy lips, soaking himself with my wetness there.

"Please," I beg, as he notches himself against my ass.

"Oh, you ask so nicely, *stellina*," he says, his voice silken sin. And then he slowly presses against my puckered asshole, sliding into me inch by tight inch.

He gives me only enough time to accept him as my body stretches to accommodate his size. I whimper once he's fully seated in both pleasure and pain. I hate he can make my body feel this way. Every touch ignites a fire, even as I want to hurt him for his every liberty.

Instead of angling me forward on the seat, he arches me up and anchors his arm underneath my breasts. His lips land on my neck as he starts a slow grind into my ass.

"I can smell myself on your skin. Taste myself. And yet, I want more. I need my marks on your body, my name on your lips. I fucking need you, Celia."

I squeeze my eyes closed, tears sliding down my cheeks, but I don't know if it's the shame from the orgasm building against my will or the fear he's never going to stop.

"Say my name, say Nic as you come, *stellina*, and I'll make you feel so good the next time. I'll get on my knees for you and lick your sweet little cunt. Would you like that?" Each word is punctuated with an arch of his hips into my body.

Everything in me is coiled tight, ready to explode, and I'm trying with all my might to hold back, to keep from coming, because if I do, it feels like he's won.

And when he wins, I always lose.

I close my eyes against another wave of sensations that slowly build like flames in a fireplace. One tiny nudge, and I'll go over.

A flicker of motion from the front seat causes Nicolo to grip me tighter against him.

His voice is entirely different when he speaks to the driver. "If you so much as glance back here again, I'll blow your head off and use it for bowling practice. Then I'll fuck her using your blood as lube while I do it."

A skitter of fear coils through me at the dark menace rolling off him. A few seconds of stillness pass until he loosens his grip a bit and starts rocking into me faster.

I'm afraid to move, to look at him, to hold on to the seat, to keep my balance even as my knees ache from the position.

It hurts, and it feels good, and I hate him. God, I hate him. I hate him so fucking much that I think my hate is becoming something else entirely.

I make it a mantra in my head as he moves faster inside me, pumping into me harder as my body gives way to his.

"Say my name, *stellina*. I want to hear it. Say it, and I'll grant you one wish as long as it's not your freedom or Lucas's."

He captures my chin and tilts my head back so he can look into my eyes as he fucks me. "Say it. Fucking say it. I can feel you tightening around me. You're fighting it, but you're going to come any second, and I want to hear my name when you do. I want you to acknowledge who is giving you pleasure even as you complain about me fucking you against your will."

I squeeze my lips together defiantly, refusing to give in. This is one thing he can't force from me. He can own my body and make me feel whatever he wants, but he can't make me speak. He can't make me think or believe what he has to say.

"Fine," he growls into my ear, then shoves me flat onto the seat and starts a furious pace, slamming into me hard and fast.

I'm about to come. The orgasm builds higher and higher, and I wrap my fingers around the warm leather of the seat to anchor myself. But right before my body explodes, he jerks himself from my ass and spills his cum all over my ass and lower back.

I pop my eyes open, my body strung tight like a bowstring.

When his heavy panting stops and he stills above me, I risk a glance back.

"I told you to give me what I want, *stellina*, and I'll make you feel good. As I said before, I don't reward brats who don't follow orders.

After he tucks himself into his pants, he lifts me gently from the seat and settles me naked across his lap. Everything aches, and I hate I want him to finish me off, or worse, that I need it. Taking mercy on me, he tucks his hand between my thighs and tilts my chin to force our gazes together. His blue gaze bleeds into mine.

"I know you need to come, so use my hand. Rock against it. I won't help you; you'll have to do it all on your own."

When I set my jaw, he chuckles, brings his fingers to his lips, and licks them. "Mmm. I look forward to tasting you once I get you settled at home."

Exhaustion falls over me in a wave, dragging me under. I don't even realize I've settled my head against his shoulder, and he's wrapped his arms around me to keep me warm. I can think about that later.

Right now, sleep is tugging me in deep, and I don't have it in me to worry about what it all means. Not the gentle whispers he presses into my neck with fluttering kisses, nor the soft, soothing brush of his hand through the trailing ends of my hair.

Especially not the fact that I want him inside me more than anything else.

7

NIC

*W*hen we arrive at the house, I text the housekeeper to make sure the place is cleared out. I don't want a single soul to see her naked. Soo will handle Lucas until I'm ready to deal with him and figure out where he falls into my plans for Celia.

I cradle her against my chest, shove the car door open, and carry her out of the vehicle. The sun is rising on the horizon, sending soft light over her skin. She has bruises along her arms and her hips from my rough handling of her. A tiny part of me feels guilt, but a greater part loves to see my marks on her body. When she sees them, she'll know she's mine in every way.

I gently hug her tighter as I walk into the house. As promised, there's not a soul in sight. She stirs in my arms, and I carefully set her on her feet as I cross the entryway.

"So, we're back," she says, her tone strange.

"Go on up, and I'll be there in a moment. You look like you're going to pass out."

She shrugs and walks down the hall. Only now, I notice the slight limp in her step as she leans from one foot to the other. I should have been gentler with her, but I couldn't. Not when I just got her back. Not when I'm still aching to mark her everywhere.

"Stop," I call out.

She turns to look at me, her eyes blazing like a fire.

"My room isn't that way."

"I know. I'm going to *my* room."

She's not spending another night without me wrapped around her. "No. You'll be living in my room, so I can take care of you."

"Take care?" She scoffs at the words like it's a joke. "Like you just cared for me in the car?"

"Do you want me to carry you?"

She glares, crossing her arms over her breasts to hide them from my view. "No. I can go up to my *cell* alone. And I'm going to sleep alone and be locked up in my own space."

I saunter closer to her in case she bolts. "I never said I was locking you up."

Her eyes track up my bare chest. I forgot to put my shirt on her when we got out of the car. Or maybe I just wanted her bare skin against mine a little longer. "No? Then let me go home."

"This is your home now. The quicker you get used to the idea, the quicker you can get comfortable."

This time she advances on me, dropping her arms to square off her hips with her hands. "I don't want to get fucking comfortable. I don't know if you caught this in the car, but I fucking hate you, and I don't want to spend another second of my time in your presence."

"You don't have a choice, princess. You're in my world. What I say is law, and I decided you will be here with me indefinitely." She isn't just in my world, she is the center of it, and I'll make certain she knows that.

Taking one more step forward, she pokes at my chest with her index finger. "And what are you going to do? Bend me over a piece of furniture and stake your claim again? Carve your name in my skin, so everyone knows who owns me? Or maybe come on me every single morning to let the rest of the dogs know you've marked your territory?"

I lash out and grab her wrist harshly. "Watch your mouth, princess. I'm in a forgiving mood toward you right now because I used you hard, but it won't last if you keep running your mouth."

"What can you possibly do to hurt me you haven't already? I want to go to my room and sleep. Alone."

She tries to pry her wrist from my hold, but I grip her tighter. "You continually think you have a choice here. I told you to go to my room. If you won't go there yourself, I'll carry you up and tie you to my bed." I lean into her face and whisper my next words. "And I'm not sure if you remember, but I don't make idle threats. So, what's it going to be?"

Again, she tries to jerk her wrist from my hand. I let her go, and she stumbles back, rubbing the delicate bone. "I'm not going to lie in your bed and be your sex doll while you plot your next auction to sell me. I'd rather be left alone; at least I can enjoy the time by myself until someone else takes ownership of me."

"I told you, I'm not selling you. I'm keeping you. You're mine."

Her eyes narrow, and her jaw locks tight. "Oh, you're keeping me," she grits out. "Like a dog you found in some alley."

A familiar fucking weight settles in my chest, and I shake my head at her. "Why do you always have to twist everything I say into the worst possible connotation?"

"Because I hate you. And everything you say makes me fucking sick."

It's not that I expected her full submission when we returned to the house, but I see now, I'm going to have to reteach her to respect me, or at the very least, fear me enough to not piss me off at every turn. My woman will not humiliate me.

Soo enters from the garage hallway, keeping his eyes averted. He's the only person in the world who can be in the same room with her naked and survive.

"He's secure. I thought you'd want to know, and you weren't answering your text messages."

I wave at Celia. "It's because I'm dealing with the princess here who has forgotten how to follow my orders."

Soo, tactfully, gives me a nod and turns back to the hallway to wait until I've finished handling things with her.

I stare down at her, my blood rising. The need to grab her and take her again, shimmering under the surface. "I'm going to give you one last chance. Go up to my room, or I'll drag you up there myself, and I won't be gentle about it. That is the choice I'm giving you. A choice you can make."

Glowering at me like she wants to drive a knife into my chest, she squares her shoulders and stands her ground. I know her pride won't allow her to bend even as she stares me down naked with her hands shaking, trying her best to cover herself.

I grab her by the throat and drag her to me so her mouth can feel each word I say. "You have no idea what I've given up for you. I gave up my chance to get to your father. A revenge I've planned for many years... I gave it up so I could find you. And yet, you stand here ungrateful and defiant. I'll teach you how to act if it kills us both."

"I didn't ask you to find me. I was perfectly fine where I was."

"Is that right? So, Lucas had a knife against your throat for fun?"

I switch my hold to the back of her neck and shove her ahead of me toward the stairs. She stumbles, but I take her arm so she doesn't fall and lead her up to the bedrooms. It only takes a few minutes to enter my darkened room and march her straight to the bed. When she doesn't climb on, I easily lift her and toss her onto the bed.

Of course, she doesn't stay. She shuffles across the bed to the other side and scrambles over the edge to the floor.

I take a moment to watch her and shake my head. "Why do you fight when it's so easy to just give in?"

With her scent still on me, I'm calmer now. The need to drag her by the hair like a caveman still lingers, but I can hold it back until she pushes me too far.

When she reaches the door, I make it to the threshold first and drag her by the waist, her back crashing against my front. "I told you your options, and by refusing to behave, you're just ensuring future punishment. Stay on the fucking bed, or I'll tie you there. When I come back, if you've even moved an inch, I'll make you regret it."

She claws at my arms with her nails. "There is nothing else you can take from me."

I nuzzle against her ear. "Princess, I haven't even tapped into my imagination. There are so many ways to make you mine, and I'll use them all until you submit."

She shudders and goes limp.

"Good girl," I whisper and carry her back to the bed.

This time when I deposit her on the covers, she stays put. I don't trust she'll stay, so I wait, watching her for any sign she's about to run again.

"Why are you standing there watching me?"

"Because I don't trust you to follow directions."

She pulls the blanket up over her lap and then up to cover her chest. "Am I allowed to use the restroom and take a shower?"

I shake my head. "Not unless I'm with you. Not until I know you won't do something stupid. Right now, I've got business to attend to regarding the fallout from last night's auction, so I'm going to need to leave you here. I'm just waiting to see if you'll need to be tied up or not."

Her lips press into a firm line, and she looks so pretty in nothing but my blankets. I want to press her into the mattress and feast on her. But that kind of treatment is for good girls, and Celia is testing me at every turn.

"So, what's it going to be?" I ask, still studying her.

I love the pink flush dotting the creamy skin across her breasts. My cum is there right now, marking her as mine, and I don't stop the smile that blooms on my lips.

Her heavy gulp echoes through the silent room. Even as she acts brave and ballsy, she's terrified. I can smell her fear, taste it, and soon she'll be brave and ballsy when I want her to be, and terrified when I want her to be, and mine the second I say the word.

The image of her in my head, twining around me voluntarily, enjoying my touch, and touching me in return is too much. My cock is already hardening despite coming twice in the car. She is a fucking drug I can't seem to get enough of.

"Answer me, *stellina*. I can't stand here all morning. Soo is waiting for me."

In another act of defiance, she drags her gaze from mine and clamps her mouth shut. Fine. Tied up, it is.

I climb onto the bed and grab her wrist in one smooth move. She claws at my ribs, trying to escape as I yank my still unbuckled belt from its loops to restrain her against the heavy wooden headboard. Once her arm is secure, I retrieve another belt and loop it around her other wrist. Tight enough, she can't get free.

Then I lean in and brush her mouth with my own. She tries to bite me, but I grip her chin and force her mouth shut. "Remember what I said about biting. Since you wanted to take your time about your decision, I made it for you. Next time, maybe you'll be more expeditious. Now, I'm going downstairs. You get some sleep, and I'll release you in a few hours, so you can get some breakfast."

Before I go, I delve my other hand down her body to dip my fingers into her pussy. She gasps and jerks her hips into the bed, but she can't escape. Her cunt is still wet, and I know a few deliberate motions would make her come. I'm not giving that to her yet, not until she's earned it.

I lick my fingers and close my eyes as I taste her. A tiny squeak pops out of her, and I can't help but smile. She might pretend she doesn't want me, but she does, desperately.

"I'll be back in a few hours," I repeat. "Get some rest. You're going to need it."

I enter my closet and grab a T-shirt before heading into the hallway. Soo is standing with his back against the wall, looking just as tired as I feel.

"We need to talk," he says.

I tug the hem of the shirt down and start walking toward my office. He follows.

"What is it?" I ask once we get inside the room.

"Some of the bidders at the event are trash talking you and the services we provide. It's not a good look for us."

Shit. I anticipated that we'd see some blowback from losing her, but I didn't expect it to be so fast. Nor to occur before I had the chance to either kill some people or bribe them into silence.

"Who's complaining?"

Soo throws himself into the chair in front of my desk and bends over to cradle his head. It's been a long night for both of us. "The buyer. He's complaining about losing his prize and is promising to retrieve her himself."

The singular thought of another man touching or even attempting to touch her reignites the rage Celia's body only just cooled.

"I'd love to see him try." I snicker. "He got his money back, so I don't know what he is complaining about. Let's wait for him to make his move. Then, at the very least, I'll have a legitimate reason to kill him."

8

CELIA

Somehow, I manage to get a few hours of sleep. Probably by sheer exhaustion. When I wake sometime later, my wrists ache, and my fingers are numb from being secured to Nicolo's bed for hours. That's not all I wake to. There is a blanket of warmth surrounding me from my neck down to my toes.

I blink my eyes a few times to adjust to the light and find Nicolo passed out, his naked body cupped to the side of my own.

It's more of a shock to find him naked. Every time he takes off clothes, it's mostly just shoving them aside than taking them off; he's never been fully nude in front of me. The muscles low in my belly tighten at the image before me. Why do I like it so much? He's solid, strong, his muscles dip and rise under his skin. Looking at him gives me the strange urge to trace the ridges of him with my teeth and tongue, to learn the map of his body just as he's surely memorized mine.

It's nothing. Obviously, I'm still on edge from him denying me an orgasm this morning. That has to be the only reason I find him so appealing right now. It's definitely not the inky black tattoos tracking over his skin or the faint dusting of hair leading from his belly button down to his semi-erect cock. The man is always hard when he's around me.

He stirs beside me, and I quickly stare up at the ceiling. I can't have him thinking I actually want him.

"My *stellina*..." he whispers against my neck, his breath raising goose bumps down my bare chest.

I keep silent and wiggle my wrists, hoping he gets the hint. He grunts and unbuckles the belts, gently lowering my arms to the bed. I can't move my wrists or my fingers, and an intense tingle builds in my muscles as he lies there and massages my wrists, palms, and fingers so gently. It's like he can be the kindest man ever, and in a flash, he can become the monster of your worst nightmare.

"Better?" he asks.

I tug my hands from his grasp and rotate each wrist to make sure the circulation is restored. As much as I want to fight him at every turn, I don't want to spend another night tied to his bed. It's my own fault. I know he always follows through on a threat. I was just too angry to care, too full of pride.

"Are you hungry?" he asks, his voice deep and sleep ridden.

The sound tugs low in my belly, and I shake my head. "No, not yet. I really need to use the restroom and take a shower."

He hops off the bed like a true morning person, and I scowl at his stupidly nice bare ass. When he comes around and holds his hands out to me, I glare at them. "I can get up by myself."

To my surprise, he doesn't argue, just walks into the bathroom. I'm ashamed to admit I watch his ass until it disappears.

While he's brushing his teeth, I gingerly climb off the bed. I'm sore all over from the Diavolo brothers' manhandling of me most of the last twenty-four hours. I look down at my body. Bruises line my hips, my wrists, and my upper arms.

They are minor, though, so I rub them gently but resolve to ignore them. They will always heal. It's the deeper stuff that never goes away.

Nic's standing in the doorway when I arrive.

"Excuse me," I say.

He shifts to the side to let me pass, and I squeeze through and head to the toilet. He doesn't leave as I turn around to sit, and I'm confused why he's still standing there.

"You can go."

His shrug sends my belly to my toes. "I'm not going anywhere. You haven't eaten in, I don't know how long, and you're a little unsteady on your feet. I won't let anything happen to you. As I said, you belong to me. I'm responsible for your care in every way."

I have to pee, and it's not worth arguing about this, so I sit and make direct eye contact while I take care of my needs. He just stares back with a grin on his stupidly handsome face. When I finish and wash my hands, I glance at the large shower stall. "Are you going to stay while I shower, too?"

He brushes past me and turns on the water, testing the temperature every few seconds. "Is that good?"

I stick my hand under the spray and shake my head. "I like it hotter."

He shrugs like he doesn't care and cranks up the temperature. Once it's where I like it, I step under the spray, and he follows me, crowding against my back.

"I can do this on my own."

He tips my head back into the water and strokes my scalp into the spray. "I know you can shower yourself, but I'm taking care of you now. And you will have no secrets from me. I'll assist you when I feel like it, and I'll watch you when I want to."

I should argue with him about his control issues, but I can't think as he massages shampoo into my scalp with his strong fingers. It takes everything in me not to moan out loud, between his hands and his slick, desirable body aligned with mine. Warm heat coils in my belly.

After he rinses my hair, he adds conditioner and tugs me out from under the direct spray. His gaze takes on a predatory gleam as he soaps up a washcloth. He stares down at my body like he can't quite decide where to start. He gently washes my bruised wrists first, and then, just as carefully, runs the washcloth over every inch of me, even between my toes and behind my ears. I don't think I've ever been so thoroughly soaped up.

He rinses me with equal care from the soap to the conditioner. I'm practically a big ball of goo by the time he slides the glass door open.

And as if I'm in some posh spa, he produces two large fluffy, warm towels and wraps me up. "Thank you," I whisper.

He leads me back into the bedroom, plants me on the bed, climbs up behind me, and gently starts running a brush through my hair.

I can't take it anymore. This has to stop. "What are you doing?"

The brush slides along my scalp, shooting tingles down my spine.

"Taking care of you."

"But why? Why are you doing this? I can care for myself, and I'm sure you have plenty of bad guy things you could be doing. You know, like ruining people's lives and kidnapping people?"

"Nope. The only life I have to ruin today is yours. Soo is taking care of a few things, and I'll touch base with him later. Do you want me to call down and have Sarah bring some food up for us?"

I don't want to admit I want anything from him, but I'm so hungry my stomach is cramping up. Biting back my words, I nod.

He grabs his phone from the bedside table and types out a text. Then resumes his grooming of me. After a short while, I'm reminded that I still don't know what is going to happen next. Where do we go from here?

"So, you are keeping me until you get bored or until I say something that pisses you off?"

He snorts. "I'm pretty sure you say more that pisses me off than you do otherwise."

I can't wrap my head around what he's saying. If he doesn't want to sell me, then what does he want to do with me? And when did I suddenly start caring? The last two days have me upside down and turned inside out. I was sure when he left me in that room, and we parted ways, I'd never see him again, let alone ever hear him say that I belong to him, in more than a form of revenge. This is different. His need for me hinges on something deeper.

"Then please just tell me what you want?" My tone is calm, level, and I hope we can have a civil conversation for once. Ours always seem to develop into a fight, or worse.

His hands go still in my hair. "I want you. That's it." He pauses, "No, that's not it. I want you to want me in return. And while I can understand that, it might take you some time to come around to that. I'm willing to wait."

I blink and pull away from him, turning fully so I can actually look at his face. I can't believe what I'm hearing. His features are serious, set in hard lines, and his full lips tilt down as he stares at me with the same fury I feel. Daring me to fight him, to call him names, or lash out.

Part of me feels guilt for taking advantage of his current mood, and his request, but I can't pass up the opportunity. "Is Lucas okay?"

He spins me to face away again, so he can finish brushing and drying my hair. "He is alive and should remain so if he does no more stupid shit."

"Can I see him?" I whisper.

The brush snags on a tangle, and I wince.

"No, you can't see him. Not yet."

"Not even to see if he's actually alive?"

"Really, *stellina*? You don't trust me? I'm wounded."

I jerk myself from his hands and turn around once more. "I just wanted to make sure."

He sits the brush on the bed with a long sigh. I can't help but stare at him. I've never seen him like this. And every moment since I woke up feels important somehow. And because of it, there's an extra layer of pressure not to fuck things up.

"Tell me why you care. Why it's so important to you."

Again, I'm shocked at his rational request. He seems to be a different man, and I don't understand if he's been like this all along or if he's just changed overnight. "I told you everything I knew last night. He knows something about me, about my family, and I want answers."

He tips his head to the side to study me, tracing my cheeks, down my neck to where the towel is wrapped securely above my breasts. "That's not enough. I don't want you near him, or any man." His tone is strained, like he's moderating it for my benefit. And hell, he's been strange all morning, acting like he actually cares about me. What a ridiculous idea.

I tug the towel higher and slide off the bed to look down at him. "What the hell is this? Why are you keeping me here? Is this just another level on your twisted game of revenge? Make me care so you can break me in a new fun way? Sell me as broken and a virgin?"

He shifts his legs from underneath him, and I get a full-on look at every inch of his naked body. The smirk on his face tells me how much he likes it. "I told you I wasn't going to sell you. If you bring it up again, I'm going to get angry."

"Wouldn't want you to get angry," I murmur sarcastically. "And your revenge plan to destroy everyone I love? I assume that's still on the table."

His shoulders stiffen, and he sits up straight. "You don't know anything about my plans for your father. But trust me, when I get to him, he'll pay for his sins. That, however, has nothing to do with you. I've changed my tactic. I'll find a way to hurt your father without using you. "

I wave at him. "You think I'll be able to touch you, to look at you, after you've murdered my family? Did you consider that angle in your grand plan for things?"

A knock on the door interrupts us, and he hops off the bed and opens it. A few seconds later, he turns back to face me with a tray of food. "Let's talk about this later so you can eat."

"I don't want to fucking eat. I want answers. I want you to understand how much all of this hurts me. We might not be a loving family, but they are still my parents. The only family I've ever known. Every second you plot and plan against my family is like a punch to my heart."

He carefully sits the tray on the bed and faces me, hands on his hips. "I didn't ask for your opinion, and I don't want it. If I desire to know how you feel about my murdering your family one by one, then I'll fucking ask. Until then, sit the fuck down and eat."

I swallow against the lump lodged in my throat. Obviously, his good mood couldn't last forever. And he and I have a way of butting heads. Every time we fight, things get out of hand, and I step away from him, waiting for when he's had enough of my mouth and makes a move to shut me up.

"I was just trying to be honest with you, but as I thought, you want a sex doll, not an actual woman with thoughts and feelings."

He stalks forward, and I jerk away from him. When he drops his hands, I dare to meet his eyes. My knees are already trembling in anticipation of whatever violence I'm luring out of him.

"You aren't being honest. How can you be when you don't know the entire story?" he says.

I wait for him to elaborate, but he doesn't. "And what, I don't deserve that either?"

Again, he charges forward, and I tuck my chin, trying to anticipate how he's going to grab me and what he's going to use to punish me this time.

Shock consumes me when he gently cups the back of my head and draws me into him slowly. I don't resist, still coiled, waiting for him to strike.

He leads me to the bed, sits down, and gathers me, towel and all, across his lap. I freeze in his grip, waiting for something. All he does is hug me to his chest, and after a moment, he scoops my hair to the back of my neck and presses his forehead into mine.

"I'm going to be hard on you. Some days, I'll be so demanding you won't be able to stand it. Others, I'll care for you so gently you'll be putty in my hands. And even still, there will be days you hate the very sight of me. But the thing you need to remember is no matter how bad or good the days are, you belong to me."

His tone takes on an edge, and the grip on my neck tightens as he digs his fingers into my skin. "You belong to me," he repeats. "Every breath you take is mine. Every time you fall apart, every happy moment, and sad, they all belong to me. One day you'll understand, but for now, just know you're safe. I won't be selling you. No one will gawk at you or touch you except me."

I swallow heavily, my heart beating hard against my ribs, and I don't even know why. It's not like I want him. Because I don't. I definitely want nothing to do with this murderer who turns me inside out and makes me feel every nerve ending in my body.

He tugs the tray toward him on the bed and lifts a piece of toast to my lips. "Eat for me."

And all I can do is meet his eyes and let him feed me.

9

NIC

There's an accusation in her eyes. As if I've stolen her all over again, and she's counting the seconds until she can break free. I hate that the look is there because of me, but I'm also not strong enough to give her up. Not strong enough to watch her slip from my grasp.

She frowns as I feed her a bite of scrambled eggs. In her mind, feeding her is an act of degradation. In mine, it's an act of caring, an act of a provider.

When she finishes chewing, I feed her a bit of sausage and take a bite for myself.

"Why are you doing this?"

Deliberately misunderstanding her question, I say, "You're hungry, and I want to feed you."

"That's not what I meant, and you know it."

I hold the fork up to her lips again, but she bats my hand away and shakes her head.

"Not eating isn't going to help your situation. You might as well enjoy my excellent cook as part of the perks."

Her scowl makes me grin as I move the tray to my dresser and then return to the bed.

"Now what?" she asks, ice returning to her voice.

I tuck a piece of damp hair behind one of her delicate ears. "I give you what you tried to offer me before the auction, a way to ensure you don't get put on the block again, by me or anyone else."

"How?" Her eyes narrow in suspicion.

My grin should be a warning, but her eyes are still wide as I tug the tucked ends of the towel around her breasts and strip it away.

She tries to chase after the towel, but I've already jerked it off and tossed it on the floor before she can get a proper grasp on the cotton.

"What the hell? I don't want to sleep with you," she whines, cupping her hands over the breasts I just carefully washed.

"It's adorable that you think you have a choice, princess. Do you want your buyer to get his hands on you? Because I promise, if he finds you, and you're still a virgin, he's going to be a very happy man until he breaks you and then discards you."

"How is that different from what you're doing to me?"

I wave at the food and toward the shower. "I'm caring for you. Having sex with you, while I admit, will be enjoyable, is also meant to ensure you lose some of your appeal to many of my clients in the future."

Her gaze is even icier than her tone now. "How magnanimous of you to fuck me to keep me safe. What a hardship this must be for you."

With a snatch, I grasp her chin and pull her into me. "Watch your tone, *stellina*. I'm being gentle with you, but I won't be disrespected so defiantly."

She clamps her mouth shut and continues to glare. I can't wait to wipe that look from her eyes when I make her shudder and moan around my cock.

"Come here," I say and drag her naked into my lap. Her ass is full and soft in my hands, and I knead my fingertips into her muscles.

Thankfully, she doesn't fight, her body straddling mine, her knees pinned against my hips. Her core is flush with my already lengthening erection, and I watch her until she realizes, her body tightening above mine as if she wants to pull away but can't think of how to do it safely.

"Are you nervous?" I ask, curious about what she is thinking regarding my plan.

She shakes her head a little too hard to be the truth.

I trail my lips over the tight curve of her jaw and enjoy the way she squirms against me. "Don't worry. I'll take care of you."

Carefully, I cup her ass in my hands and roll us over, so she's flat on her back, and I'm wedged between her thighs. She sucks in a ragged breath that is loud between us.

"I'm not going to just take you. I have to make sure you're ready first. I'll try to minimize the pain the best I can. And then afterward, make sure you come so hard you see stars."

She averts her gaze and grits her teeth. "Don't bother."

Damn this woman and her pride. I drag her chin down to force her to look at me. "Did you just say 'don't bother?' Because if that's the case, then I shouldn't. I should push you so very close and leave you trembling on the edge, just like I did in the car. Do you want that?"

Her head shake is minimal, but I know I've gotten inside.

"Then fucking change your tune. Tell me you want me to make you come, and I'll forget what a mouthy little brat you are."

The clench in her jaw and the fire in her glare are the only outward signs of her anger toward me. I'll take it. Anger is a thousand times better than indifference.

I lean in and wet my lips, my tongue touching her mouth. Then I say, "Tell me, and I'll be forgiving. This time."

Her lips follow mine as I slowly pull away. She wants me more than she's willing to let me see, and I can work with that. But I won't always. Soon she's going to be taking my cock daily and with fucking gratitude.

"I'll make you a deal," I add. "I'll get started here, and you have until I come to say those words, and I'll still be generous and give you an orgasm. If you don't, well, I'll finish, clean you up, and tie you to the bed again until you learn how to overcome that damn pride of yours."

She doesn't answer me, and that's fine. I'll have her begging soon enough. It's the future I'm worried about. I plan to keep her, and if she can't tell me what she wants, how is she ever going to get it? Especially when she hides her needs behind her ego.

I reach between us and part her nether lips, so I can slide my length along the slickness already gathered there. Fuck, she's already hot and wet. The memories from earlier this morning charge back in my mind, threatening my control.

She hisses against my mouth, and I catch it in a kiss. The taste of eggs and something all around her teases me. Her fingers thread up around my neck, and I let her lead for a heartbeat, just to see how far she'll go. When she thrusts her tongue between my lips, I arch upward again, so the head of my cock runs across her slippery clit. She's so damn wet already. And it's all for me. All mine.

The whimper she lets out earns her lips a gentle nip with my teeth. "You like that. Want me to do it again?"

She nods, her forehead brushing mine with each assent. Because she's actually telling me, I shift my hips and glide along her clit once more. It's not as good as being inside her, but it still drives me closer to my orgasm.

Leaving a lingering kiss on her lips, and bracing myself off her body, I resettle with my mouth at the apex of her thighs.

My fingers sink into her thighs and I drag her to my mouth. Burying my face in her pussy, I inhale, letting her scent fill my lungs. *Mine, all fucking mine.* The words echo inside my mind. Parting her folds, I find her tiny clit and lick the nub until her legs are shaking, and she's panting.

Then I focus on her opening, dipping my tongue in and out, fucking her with it, delving into her sweet honey while she tries to rock forward and fuck my face.

"You taste so sweet," I murmur between strokes of my tongue.

She protests my pause and continues to grind against my mouth. I let out a chuckle and wrap my arms around her upper thighs to hold her down while I spear her with my tongue, fucking her little hole until I'm so hard I can't wait any longer. She's more than ready for me as her arousal glistens on her thighs.

She lets out another whimper when I pull away and reposition myself so I'm kneeling between her legs. Our gazes collide, fire and ice become one, clashing together. I bring two fingers to her entrance and press deep inside her channel, all the way to my knuckles. Warm and so fucking tight. I'm aching to get inside her. Every inch of my cock is primed to fucking claim her and make her mine in every way.

The idea of being the first man here, the only man here, lights up something primal in my chest. It makes me want to growl and grunt with satisfaction. She's fucking mine, and this is proof even to her, even in the moments when she wants to deny me.

Slowly, I stroke her from the inside out, enjoying the way her eyes light up with every pump of my fingers. My queen likes her pleasure with a splash of pain, but tonight will be different. I pump into her a few more times for safe measure and stretch her tightness to prepare her for my girth. As much as I want to sink into her and fuck her straight through the mattress, I know I need to go slow to make certain she enjoys it. That we both do.

"Are you ready?" I shift forward and glide my cock through her wetness, circling her clit with the head before delving back down to prod gently at her opening. She doesn't pull away, and instead arches her hips, trying to take me before I'm ready.

"I want you." She frowns when I deny her.

It earns her a swat on her hip with my free hand. "Patience, *stellina*. I'll give you what you want when I'm ready."

Her frustrated huff makes me smile as I climb back up and brace the weight of my body on my forearms.

"Are you ready now?" she asks, her voice full of sweet venom.

I surprise her when I nip her lip before she even realizes it's happening. "Greedy brat, big words from someone who still hasn't told me she wants me to make her come."

"You're an asshole."

I slide along her slickness once again, groaning into her neck, and she throws her head back, offering herself to me.

Gently, I nibble a line from her chin to her collarbone. "An asshole you want inside you more than you want anything else right now. Be nice, or I won't let you have my cock."

When she flexes her fingers around my biceps in frustration, I decide to show her some mercy. I lean my weight on one arm and reach between us to guide my cock to her entrance. Pressing between her thighs, the heat of her body engulfs me.

With my lips against her forehead, I thrust my hips forward, gently. A fucking feat, since all I can think about is slamming home and taking her hard.

The head of my cock slips inside her tight hole, and sheer bliss blankets every inch of my body. I grapple for control, and it takes every shred I have left to stop myself from thrusting all the way inside.

Celia's whimper fills my ears, and that sound alone grounds me. Carefully, inch by inch, I feed my cock inside her. Every time her fingernails dig into my skin, I pause and let her grow used to the pressure, the stretch she's surely experiencing. After what feels like an eternity and several tests of my control, I become fully seated inside her, our bodies nestled together completely.

"Are you okay?" I grit out. Determined not to fucking spill my load after two minutes inside her. She's so fucking tight, and I've never felt such perfection in my life.

She nods, her jaw tight. "I'm fine, don't stop."

Not the endorsement I want, but I know with some movement, things will ease, and pleasure will replace the pain.

I tuck my hand between our bodies again and nudge her clit with my fingers. She sucks a heavy breath into her lungs, and I know that's what she needs.

"There we go. Relax for me, let me do the work," I whisper.

Miraculously, she listens to me and relaxes her hips into the bed. It changes the angle of things, and soon enough, she's arching her hips up to meet mine with every steady thrust.

Her tight cunt is like a vice I want to get lost in.

"Remember what I said. You won't come unless you tell me."

Her eyes are squeezed closed, and her movements grow frantic. "I fucking hate you."

"No, you don't. You just wish you did," I tell her, dragging my teeth down her neck. "Say it," I order, and pray she does. I'm so close to coming, and despite my threats, I won't enjoy leaving her suspended on the edge of her orgasm.

I'd do it to teach her the lesson, but I wouldn't like it.

"I'm going to come," she grits out.

Instantly, I stop moving and even move my hands to pin her body to the bed, so she can't use me to reach her end.

She pops her eyes open to glare at me. "You are a fucking bastard."

I smile. "Then we were made for each other. Say it, and I'll make you come so fucking hard. Harder than you've ever come in your life."

Her glare could melt ice. But I welcome it, and even more so when she finally says, "I want you to make me come." My cock pulses deep inside her and I lean into her.

"Good girl," I whisper against her mouth.

Snaking my hand back between our bodies, I find her clit and pinch it hard between my index finger and thumb while I rock into her body, harder and faster than before.

Seconds is all it takes for her to break around me. Her body clenches my cock in its strong, rhythmic grip. I hold myself off, closing my eyes, focusing on her until her hips ease back to the bed. Then I move again, pounding into her harder until my orgasm rears up, and I press in to the hilt, letting the warm sheath of her body hold me as the pleasure rolls through me in waves.

I might have promised to make her come harder than she ever has in her life, but I just did, too. It takes me a moment to blink through a haze of disorientation and carefully pull from her body's embrace.

She winces as I do so, and I catch sight of the red sheen along my still semi-hard dick.

"Stay there. I'll be right back." I grab a washcloth from the bathroom, wet it with hot water, and return to press it to her pussy.

Her sigh of relief stirs something in my chest. Let alone the fact that she stayed exactly where I told her to, legs splayed, waiting for me to care for her. Maybe she is learning to take direction after all.

Once I clean her gently, I go back to the bathroom and clean myself up.

When I return to the bed, I scoop her up to the top of the bed and tuck her under the covers. She doesn't protest as I mold myself around her body and draw her into my embrace. Every inch of her is touching me, and I press a kiss to the curve of her neck as she drifts off to sleep.

She might fight how much she wants me, but inside, her body already knows it's my right to care for her. My right to keep her. My right to control her. And soon, she'll understand exactly what it means to be mine.

10

CELIA

I've been in this house for a week. One week since he touched me tenderly and then lit my body on fire from the inside out. Even now, thinking about it, I ache for him, and every day, I grow a little less ashamed of myself for it too.

I lift the neckline of Nicolo's shirt to my nose, inhaling deeply. It smells like him, like me, like sex. Like I do when I slip my fingers between my legs in the middle of the night and bring myself to orgasm at the memory of his body pressed against mine. Every time he turns those dark, haunted blue eyes on me, I should run in terror, but I'm not.

When I enter the bedroom after breakfast, a black dress bag is lying on the perfectly made bed. The maid already cleaned in here, so Nic must have left it out for me. I cross the room and stare down at the gleaming zipper.

I unzip the bag and fold back the edges. A red dress lays inside. Not like the one he gave me when he held me captive, but a deeper red, more maroon or wine-colored. I lift the hanger out and hold it up to the light. It has got a subtle shimmer to the fabric. The A-line cut will look good on me.

Sarah bustles in the door I left open with a stack of towels for the bathroom. "Pretty dress."

Since Nic made it clear I'm staying, the staff has warmed up and even deign to speak full sentences to me now. Although Sarah still acts like she couldn't care either way who I am, as long as I'm willing to clean up after myself.

"Thanks. I assume Nic left it for me."

"Well, he sure didn't leave it for me," she calls from the bathroom.

A chuckle pops out of me, and I lay it back on the bed. He didn't leave a note explaining if he wants me to save it for later, so I decide to put it on now. Why not, since it's appropriate for daytime?

I strip off the oversized T-shirt and basketball shorts I wore to break-fast and tug the dress on. Of course, the zipper is in the back, and I have to twist my arms to pull it up.

"Hold on." Sarah appears in front of me. She wipes her hands on her apron as she steps up behind me and raises the zipper to the back of my neck.

I'm a little surprised by her actions since I still think she doesn't like me, though, I'm not sure why exactly.

"Thank you," I tell her and watch her walk away without another word.

I look in the mirror. It's a beautiful dress. Not as slinky as he usually gives me, and I catch myself swishing the skirt around as I stare in the mirror.

Fuck. I'm falling into his trap. No doubt this is part of his plan. Make me too comfortable, so comfortable I don't want to leave, and then he has me forever.

Every time he listens when I say no. Each tender caress and compliment, all carefully designed to draw me out and push my guard down.

He carefully designed every step to ensure I forget... I'm his prey.

Suddenly, the bedroom walls close in on me, and I need to escape.

I keep the dress on and head out into the hallway. No one is around. Nic is likely in his office, working on whatever it is he does. I head toward the library but almost run into Soo as he comes around the corner, no doubt on his way to see Nic.

"Nice dress," he says. "Aren't you supposed to be staying in the room?"

I shrug. "I felt trapped in there. I just wanted to go to the library and find a book."

He nods and studies me, his gaze scanning me from head to toe. I'm not sure what he's hunting for, but after a moment, he drags his gaze back to my eyes and nods. "He certainly likes you in red."

I noticed that. "What's not to like?"

His laugh surprises me. "Indeed. It's a lovely color, and you do it justice."

As always, he toes the line of propriety and familiarity. Never wanting to walk too close to a point Nic might object to.

After that awkward encounter, I continue to the library, and he heads off toward Nic's office. No doubt he will tell him I've left the room, so I probably only have a few solitary minutes to find a book and go back.

The hard part is I'm torn between following his orders, embracing the possibilities of what he is offering, and running as far and fast as possible. The conflict is the worst part. Every morning the uncertainty eats at me, gnawing on my gut, waiting for me to make my choice.

When I enter the library, a light breeze wafts in from the open balcony doors. I cross the room and stare out into the morning light. It smells like rain, a heavy ozone scent hanging in the air. It feels good to be outside, so I step further onto the patio until my toes meet the soft blades of grass.

I take another step, and then another, and before I can truly think about my actions, I'm racing across the grass, digging my toes into the soft earth. There are acres of lawns around his house, and I don't see any fence lines or cars in the distance. I'd somehow made the choice, and now I don't know where I'm going.

I'm one heavy exhale away from stopping, turning around, and going back when someone takes me down onto the lawn from behind. A tackle, but I land on top of Nic's chest instead of on the ground. The air is knocked out of me, and I drag in a heavy inhale. It takes a moment to get my bearings, my head spinning from the jostling impact with his hard chest.

I shove up to straddle him, and his jaw is set, his eyes hard. "Where were you going to go?"

Instead of lying, I shrug. "I don't know. It wasn't really something I thought through that time. I walked outside, and then I kept going."

He rolls us over, so I'm trapped under the heavy, solid weight of him. A weight I find more and more comfortable every time we end up in this position.

I'm bracing for his anger, for his harsh words, but he simply stares down at me. "You can't leave."

"I got that from the running tackle I just took," I say, trying to soften my tone with a smile on the end.

He doesn't give me anything in return but another hard look. "No, really. If you leave, I don't know what would happen. Not only is it unsafe for you, but I don't know what I'll do if I don't have you."

I rub my fingers against his temple and meet his eyes, trying to discern what he is saying between the threats. I'm learning he gravitates to threats and violence when things get emotional for him. "You think someone will try to take me?"

He nods. "Besides your family, I know of one other person who would love to get his hands on you. And those don't include my enemies, who would be overjoyed to learn of your existence in my life. A weakness."

I don't like the way he says that. "A weakness?"

Something shifts in his gaze. And suddenly, I'm not staring at the man but the predator. His hips are pressed into mine, and he's rocking into me gently, the dress bunched up around my hips.

"If you leave, I can't guarantee the safety of anyone. Not your family, not Lucas, none of them," he growls out, his mouth only a few inches from mine.

And we are back to threats. We made it a week of semi-normalcy, and now he reverts to his baser instincts to ensure I stay with him. No matter how many times I tell him holding me captive does not make me his girlfriend.

His fingers curl around my neck gently, not squeezing but claiming, owning. "You belong to me."

"So, you keep saying," I whisper, dropping my hands from where they were massaging his head. If he's going to start with this shit, then I'm not going to touch him voluntarily.

The wetness from the grass is seeping into the back of the dress, and I hope it's not stained. But knowing him, by the time he's finished asserting his claim again, it will be.

"What do you want from me, Nic? I was about to turn around and go back inside. I'm not leaving. Hell, I don't even have any shoes on. Where do you think I'd go?"

He tracks his eyes over my face, hunting the lie in my words. But there isn't one to find this time. But no doubt he can hear the disappointment, the exhaustion of our situation, and this damn hamster wheel we keep spinning on.

"So, were all the pretty words and fancy clothes a lie? A way for you to assert your control over me?"

A line appears on his forehead, and he releases my neck. "No."

"And you being gentle with me. Making me come every time we are intimate. Every pretty line you feed me while you're inside me, were all those lies?"

He blinks heavily and rears up like he doesn't enjoy the way this conversation is going. Good. That makes two of us.

"I didn't lie to you."

I force out a breath and shove at his chest. Of course, he doesn't budge. "Then why the hell are you lying on top of me, threatening me and other people again to ensure I stay? What the hell happened to you wanting me to want you? To wanting me to come to your bed willingly? If you keep this shit up, I promise you I won't be in your bed unless you drag me there."

As if the man's never had a scolding in his life, he scowls down at me, rather like a little boy who just got his favorite toy confiscated. "Understand, you belong to me, and I'll do anything to keep you, anything. And I promise you, if you run, I'll stop at nothing to bring you back and keep you."

I shake my head and capture his cheeks in my hands. "Not sure if you know this, but that's not really how voluntary works. If you force me, it's not my choice. It can't ever be my choice until I have the option to stay or to go."

He drops his head to my shoulder and grinds into me. A heavy breath escapes as pleasure chases through me at every arch of his hips.

"I need you, please," he whispers into my neck, his lips tracing the collar of my dress.

It's the please that makes me want him in return. I dig my hands between us, unbuckle his belt, open his fly, and draw his cock out. My dress is already baring me to him. He maneuvers so he can hook my panties to the side and slide into me in one smooth, practiced stroke.

I'm still new to sex, and it takes me a moment to adjust to him. My body is straining, trying to push back against the assault.

When he gives me time, I relax, sinking my shoulders into the ground, and the sensation morphs from a tight squeeze to a heady pleasure.

"There you go, *stellina*. Take me."

I wrap my arms around his neck and drag his lips to mine. And he meets me there, crashing together, kissing me with his tongue, his teeth, his lips, all of it. When I need to break for air, he continues his steady thrust inside me and drags his lips down my neck, nibbling a path that lights me up further.

Each push of him inside me sends a spiral of pleasure along my nerves. It wasn't until he took my virginity that I understood why people make such bad decisions in the name of sex. Not that the oral or anal we had in the past was terrible, it just wasn't worth all the trouble I'd witnessed in friends and on TV.

But this. This sensation is worth everything. Every sacrifice. Every fight. Every damn minute I spend doubting him.

"Does it feel good?"

I nod because words won't come out when I'm so close to coming. And I am. My body is already coiling toward the end, and each heavy rut of his cock into me is one step closer.

I wrap my legs around his hips and rock up toward him, getting us more leverage, more sensation.

We are slapping together now, wet sounds breaking up the birdsong on the lawn. His legs shake, and I know he's going to come soon too.

"Come with me," I say.

He locks his eyes with mine and drops his forehead on mine, never faltering with his tempo.

"Ready?" he whispers.

I nod, our foreheads rolling together. And then I'm there, breaking apart around him as wave after wave of sheer bliss crashes into me. His cock feels so good as he spears me, holding himself tight into my hips, his knees shaking against my ass.

As I float down from the high, I notice my back is soaked from the grass, and a cramp has taken root in my hip. A laugh bursts out of me before I can stop it.

"Probably not the ideal time to laugh," he says, staring down into my face, a look of concern etched across his features.

I shake my head. "I'm not laughing at you. I'm just a damn mess, and it was funny how I didn't even notice until after I came."

His eyes sparkle as he pulls out of me and tucks himself back into his pants. Then he squats to lift me in his arms. "I'm taking you back to the bedroom."

I twine my hands around his neck and lean into his chest, all the soft, warm feelings after sex coursing through me. Letting me be comfortable here, right now, in this moment.

"When I leave again, please stay there. If you walk out of this house, and I can't find you, it's on you what happens."

His words detonate inside me, blowing apart the soft warmth, replacing it with fragments. Shrapnel embedding itself in my heart. A warning and a reminder.

*T*hings feel different. But Celia is still holding herself back from me even as I focus my attention on keeping her comfortable and safe.

I stare at the surface of my desk, seeing her bent over the edge as I drive into her. She's spread her soft thighs and lets me sink inside her. The train of thought dissipates as Soo saunters into my office.

"You seem to avoid me," I say, with no preamble.

He shrugs and plops into the chair across from me. "You seem to be preoccupied. I'm just trying to stay out of the way while you and Celia get whatever is happening between you settled."

"She belongs to me." I observe him, waiting for him to respond.

But I know better. Soo has a better poker face than world series poker tournament winners. "I figured as much by how you have been taking care of her."

"Do you have any opinion on the change in our circumstances?"

Another shrug as he folds his hands across his stomach. "Nope, you do you. Although if you want her to accept you in full, you might need to make some changes."

Of course, he knows exactly what I'm dealing with and the reason she refuses to give herself to me fully. "Her and I are going to have to find a middle ground because my immediate plans will not change."

Instead of addressing that little bomb, he stands and retrieves a bag he set by the door. "Here's what you asked for. I hope she likes it. And I set your reservations for tonight. Good luck."

He walks out, and I come around the desk to snag the bag off the floor.

I scribble a note to Celia and drop it on top of the white tissue inside. The dress I bought her the other day I ended up ruining. So, at the very least, I owed her another beautiful piece of fabric. Not to mention I love seeing her wear what I pick out for her. I leave the bag at our bedroom door, knowing if I go inside, I won't walk out again until after I've made her come at least twice.

Even though I'm distracted, I spend the day trying to salvage the remnants of my auction. Contacting clients and smoothing ruffled feathers. When the sun sets, I clean up in my office's bathroom and head out to the foyer.

She's standing in a pool of light from the crystal chandelier, and I stop dead in the hallway's entrance.

In another red dress, floor length with a slit up to her thigh, Celia looks stunning. Her long hair is brushed to a shine, hanging down her back, and she's painted her lips an enticing shade of red that matches her dress perfectly. She spins when she hears my shoes on the tile.

She offers me a tentative smile, and I just stare at her.

"You look incredible."

When she tucks her chin, a faint flush washing into her cheeks, I lift her chin and shake my head. "No, you don't bow your head to anyone. You hold your head up and accept the praise due to you."

My response throws her off. Her mouth pops open as she looks up at me. But she says nothing.

I hold my arm out for her to grasp. "Let's go to dinner."

THE RESTAURANT IS one I've never been to, but Soo booked it. And he's picky as fuck about his food, so it must be good. We are seated immediately, and instead of sitting across from her, I crowd into her side of the booth so we can sit closer.

The drinks arrive quickly, and I try to think of something neutral I can use to make conversation.

But while I'm thinking, she's already planned out what she wants to say. I can tell by the way she folds her hands and refolds them around the stem of her wine glass. "I want to talk to you again about your plan for revenge."

I don't want to ruin her evening or her mood, so I shake my head. "It's not up for debate or conversation."

"Are you telling me I'm not allowed to have an opinion?" She bites out, staring down into her glass.

I cup my own lowball of whiskey, knowing this date is not going to go as I originally planned. "I did not say that. You took my request not to discuss a topic as my telling you that you can't discuss any topic. I'd be thrilled to discuss anything else."

She straightens and angles toward me. "Okay, then let's talk about me leaving your house."

I sigh and shake my head. "We're outside of the house right now."

"No, I mean alone. On my own."

It's obvious she's baiting me. I just don't know if it's because she wants to have a fight or if she's hoping to push me into talking about what she wants to talk about. Either way, it won't work. While my control is notoriously thin when I'm around her, things have changed between us, and her care is now my priority.

"I'm sorry, but I can't let you go anywhere alone. Not while people out there are trying to get to you or get to me by taking you."

"Great, so you kidnap me, and now I'm even more locked down than before because you took me." Her tone is icy, and she won't look at me.

I shake my head. "I'm not trying to keep you prisoner anymore. But I have to keep you safe at all costs. If something happens to you..." I trail off, my throat tight. "To be clear, I won't allow anything to happen to you."

She exhales heavily, her shoulders slumping. "I want to believe you. And strangely, after the time we've been spending together, I even want to give you what you want from me. But I can't, not when you're keeping me from the only thing I've asked for. Not when you're keeping me confined for your own ends. How can we ever be equals?"

"Who says we'll ever be equals?" I drag her hands between mine and kiss her knuckles. "You'll be my queen. And queens are always more cared for, more respected, and more feared than their kings."

"No one will ever fear me."

I study her face. "Do you want people to fear you?" It's not a question I'd usually ask, but I'm genuinely curious about her answer. "I know you have your own injustices, your own desires for revenge."

When her jaw hardens, and she dashes her eyes away, I know I've got her. "Tell me what you're thinking. I want to know."

She clears her throat and shifts beside me again. Instead of letting her fidget, I draw her into my side, hugging her against me. "When Lucas had me at his house, he said my father killed my sister. He said that when she wouldn't marry the man he wanted and ran away, he killed her."

"What are you saying? Do you want me to confirm what he told you or tell you what you want to hear?"

"I—"

The wait staff brings our dinner and sets our plates in front of us. She clamps her mouth shut and shifts away from me to eat her food.

As the server places a basket of bread on the table, he brushes against her hand. They both jerk away, but a flash of heated anger hits me before I realize what's happening.

He must see his death in my eyes as I toss my napkin on the table and stare him down.

His sense of self-preservation is good because the man flees our table toward the kitchen. I'm two seconds from chasing after him, demanding to know if he'd done it on purpose. Even if his touch was an accident, I can't abide another man touching Celia. Not alone, not in front of me, not under any circumstances.

"Are you okay?" she asks, staring at me, her fork tucked into her plate of pasta.

A red haze has coated my vision, and I'm already climbing out the booth. She jumps up and intercepts me before I clear our table. "Stop. You can't go after that kid. It was an accident that he touched me. You don't want to hurt someone for no reason."

I stare down into her face and cup her cheek. "Him touching you is a reason to hurt him."

She shakes her head. "If you go after him, then this dinner will be ruined, and you have been working so hard to make sure it's not. Please, sit down with me. Don't go after him."

It takes effort, but the way she says please, and how her hand frames mine as I hold her face, it's enough to drag me back from the edge.

She leads me back to the table, and I take my seat beside her again.

There's still an underscore of rage simmering through me, but I ignore it for her sake.

After the interruption, we finish dinner quickly. She doesn't look like she wants to linger and share a drink with me. And why should she?

The car is waiting out front when we finish. And I instruct the driver to take us back to the house. She doesn't touch me or reach out. Even though I want to pull her into my lap and kiss her senseless, I keep my distance.

It's the hardest thing to not touch her when it's all I can think about. And while I want her obedience, I want it because she trusts me to care for her, not because she's obligated to give me it.

When we reach the house, I climb out of the car, open her door, and help her out. I offer to walk her upstairs, but we both spot Soo hovering nearby, and she shakes her head.

"No, it looks like you have some business to attend to. I'm tired anyway."

Soo crosses the foyer and intercepts us both. "I need to know what you want me to do with Lucas. He's getting restless and belligerent, and I'm about one minute from slamming his beefy little brain into the cinder block walls."

I chuckle. I can't help myself. Nothing rattles Soo, and the annoyed look on his face is priceless.

"What does he mean? What do you want to do with him?" Celia asks, a few steps away.

I tug her into my side and wrap my arm around her waist. She fits perfectly, and I love holding her here, feeling her warmth against me. It's better when she's naked, but I'll get her there soon enough.

"What does he mean? What do you want to do with Lucas?" She repeats her question.

"Ever since the night I picked you up at his house, he's been secured in our holding cell."

She gasps. "You haven't hurt him, have you?"

"Not any more than what you witnessed when I found you. I haven't exactly been in the mood to talk to him," I explain.

She drags her hands up my chest and tugs my face to look directly at her. "Please, don't hurt him. I know you guys are fighting, but he's your brother; you must have some sympathy for what he's going through."

"You're defending the man who kidnapped you."

"From an auction that the other man who kidnapped me sent me to," she snaps.

I grit my teeth and look at her. If I give her this, maybe it's the first step to breaching the distance she's created between us. This vast void she's erected to guard her heart from my grasp. "What do you think I should do with him?"

Immediately, she says, "Let him go. You punished him enough with the beating you gave him. Besides, I feel like he's being eaten alive by his guilt and his trauma. He needs help, not punishment. So, help him."

My *stellina*. Her soft heart is beautiful. I don't know how it hasn't been crushed under someone's fists by now, especially knowing what I do about her family. Her compassion should have been stripped from her by now.

She cups my cheeks, running her thumb along the bottom of my lips. I can appreciate the subtle use of her touch to entice me to give her what she wants.

I nod and look at Soo. "You heard the lady. Let him go."

Soo's face is a mask as he peers between us. All the annoyance he displayed when I arrived wiped clean. "Are you sure about that? You know there is something wrong with him right now, don't you?"

I shrug. "Talk to him. But also explain that he and I will have a conversation soon, and his continued existence will depend on those answers. And also, make sure he knows if he touches Celia again, brother or not, I'll put a bullet in his head and leave him outside for the wild animals to pick at."

Soo blinks, his only reaction to my statement. Celia goes rigid in my arms, as if she's holding her breath.

When Soo turns and heads toward the garage, I call out, "Also, maybe make sure he knows he's not to go after Ricci on his own. It'll get him killed. You and I both know he's not ready to face him, and if he tries, his emotions will ensure he ends up dead."

After Soo leaves, I focus on Celia again. "See, I can be reasonable when the request is reasonable, and the requestor is as beautiful as you are."

A soft blush washes into her cheeks. Instead of saying anything, she rocks up onto her tiptoes and presses her lips gently to mine. It's barely a kiss—more of a wish than a promise.

But I don't let her escape now that I've got her in my arms, warm and willing. "Let's go upstairs."

"For what?" she asks, all mock innocence.

I lean down and capture her mouth, demanding entrance with my tongue and then taking everything she gives me. When I allow her to come up for air, she stares at me, all heavy-lidded and pink. "Because our date isn't over until I've sunk deep inside you."

12

CELIA

I don't give myself time to rethink my plan as I stare at my reflection in the mirror. After I got up for the day and ate breakfast, I came back to the bedroom. I haven't been able to think of it as our bedroom yet, but I have an entire side of the closet and even a designated side of the bed.

Now, I'm standing in the bathroom wearing a little pink sundress. I'd found it in my closet the other day. Nic's finally been giving me clothes. He won't let me buy any myself, but at least he lets me pick from whatever he wants me to wear.

This soft dress, with spaghetti straps, hugs my body tightly, the bodice molding to my torso and then expanding to a full skirt that makes my waist look tiny.

If there's any dress to entice a man to give me what I want, this one would be it. I give my hair one last smoothing over my shoulder, and I take a deep breath to center myself. What's the worst thing that can happen? He says no, again?

I walk out of the room and head toward his office. When I poke my head in the door, he's alone at his desk, writing in his ledger.

"You can come in," he says before I even make a sound. Of course, he'd catch me lingering at his door, acting like a weirdo.

I give him a smile as I enter, walking slowly so he can look at me in the dress. His gaze tracks from my head, slowly over my breasts and down to my bare feet.

"You look beautiful. Did you come in here just to show me that dress? Because I could get used to this."

I shake my head. "No, I came to ask you a favor."

He shifts forward at his desk and studies me differently. "What do you need?"

While I walk toward him, I run over the script I made in my mind. Words I'd lined up neatly are scattered under the heated look he gives me. "Well, I want to talk to Lucas."

Immediately, he says, "No." Without even thinking about it.

"But you haven't even listened to why I want to speak to him."

He drops his gaze back to his work, and it feels like a dismissal. More than that, it grates on me. How can he look at me the way he did and then just stop?

"I don't need to listen because I've already made my decision. Not only has he betrayed my trust, but I also don't know that you will be safe with him, and I can't risk it."

I approach him, stopping at the corner of his desk. "But what if you came with me? You could make sure I'm safe, and you could monitor everything he says and does."

Again, he shakes his head. "No. I've made my decision. You're not seeing him, not until I've calmed down some from his actions, and until he shows a little remorse for what he did to you and to me."

I scoff, my anger rising. Not only because he is completely ignoring me now, but because he's still trying to control me. "That's rich. You are talking of remorse. What did he do to you, may I ask? You weren't the one who got smacked in the head, knocked out, and dragged halfway across the city."

He settles back in his chair, finally turning his gaze to mine again. "He skipped out on his responsibilities to our business, and he stole my property, which cost me millions and several clients."

"Property," I whisper.

"I've made it very clear that you belong to me."

His answer spurs me to my backup plan. I step forward, drag his hand from the edge of the desk to my hip. "Well, we could make some kind of deal, can't we?"

A smile tilts the edge of his mouth like I've finally gotten his full interest. "A deal, hmm? Are you ready to make a deal with the devil, *stellina*? I promise you; I always collect."

His tone promises dark things, all kinds of dark things I think I want.

"Well, you want me to give myself to you, so that's what I offer. You have free rein over my body. I'll do whatever you want."

"Oh, you'll do whatever I want, hmmm? Come here." He drags me onto his knee and angles me, so my legs hang between his thighs.

"Yes, anything you want." I bat my lashes and feel like an idiot trying to entice him—the man who always takes what he wants, anyway.

He laughs, and my smile wilts. "You realize that I already have free rein over your body? I can do whatever I want, anytime I want because you're mine."

"But you want me to give myself to you."

His fingers slip around the nape of my neck, and he drags our foreheads together. "Yes, I do what you to give yourself to me, but not just your body. I want your mind. I want your heart. And when you give me those things, I'll be happy. But they aren't something you're ready to give yet, as you've already told me. I doubt me granting your request will help me in that area."

"But..." My plan is crashing and burning and blowing away in the wind.

"Do you have something else to offer me?" Now, his tone is teasing, as if he's curious what else I'll say.

I jerk my head from his grip and shake my head. "What else could I possibly give you? You keep me locked up in the house. I don't have my own money, no access to the outside world. All I have is my body to bargain with."

Just saying it makes me feel dirty.

"Manipulation with sex is a nuanced business. If you want to entice me that way, you need to work on your delivery."

"I wasn't trying to manipulate you."

He tugs the hem of the dress up over my knee. "This fucking dress is one-hundred percent cotton manipulation. I want to take it off with my teeth. If I were a weaker man, you might have gotten what you want."

Now I feel guilty. I'd been trying to manipulate him, and I hate myself a little for it. "So, what do I do now then?"

He shrugs. "If you have nothing else to offer, then you lift your chin and walk away from negotiations until you have something the other party can use."

"Manipulation 101 from an expert?" I regret my words even as I say them.

His eyes go icy as he stares down at me, his fingers flexing in my hair. "I am an expert, don't forget that, *stellina*. I always get what I want when I negotiate, and I always come out ahead."

I try to tug myself off his lap, but he holds me tight, not letting me move an inch. "We aren't done talking."

"You're the one who said walk away until I can offer you something you actually want. If you don't want me, I'll go back to the bedroom."

"I didn't say I don't want you. Only that I don't need to make a deal to have you."

I jerk my chin up and level him with a glare. "What do you want, then? What's out there that you, a man with everything, might want?"

In a hard voice, he says, "Your father's head on a spike in my front lawn."

It takes a moment for his words to sink in, and then I gasp. "No, why would you say that to me?"

"It's not a secret. You're very aware of how much I want your father dead. Pretending I'm a good man won't change the fact that soon I'll murder him and get the vengeance I've been waiting years to acquire."

Again, I try to climb off his lap, but he refuses to let me leave. "Let me go. I'm done talking about this."

He hugs me against him tighter, making me gasp. "No. We are going to talk about this because you've been avoiding the discussion, and I won't let it come between us."

"It's coming between us right now. I told you I can never give you what you want while you keep dreaming about murdering my father. Even if he deserves it. When I look at you, all I'll see is his blood on your hands."

"How about we review the blood on your father's hands?" He nuzzles his face into my neck and delivers a kiss there. "How about we review the fact that he murdered my parents and my oldest brother in cold blood while my youngest brother watched? Tell me how it's any different? I don't look at you and see his blood running through your veins. Your relationship to him isn't stopping me from making you mine."

His words make me consider, for the first time, his actions balanced with my father's. It would be so easy to call him a liar, to believe that he's spinning tales to make me hate my father for whatever nefarious purpose he's cooked up.

But none of it matters because the facts remain. He wants to kill my father, and I won't be able to look at him if he does it. Not without my answers. Besides, his professing ownership of me every five minutes doesn't say he cares, only that he likes to lay claim. He likes to own people, and for people to owe him. More than anything, he enjoys the power of his position, even if he doesn't rub it in other's faces.

"You only want me for right now. I'm a novelty to you, revenge, as you said before. When I look at you, I see how much you want me, but it won't be long until you get bored and cast me aside. Where will I be then?"

I get a pang of guilt for saying it, but I shove it down and meet him square in the eye. "You like the idea of owning me. Of owning your enemy's daughter. It doesn't mean you want me or even know anything about me."

"You're right. I don't know anything about you. Tell me something."

I shove at his chest, but of course, he doesn't budge. "No. You don't get to pretend to care when I call you on your bullshit, either. The only thing you want from me is obedience. You want me to say yes and spread my legs. But that's it."

The look on his face would have scared me a few days ago. Now it only makes me angry.

"Have I not made you comfortable? Have I not tried to engage you in conversation? You're the one who keeps bringing up Lucas, or your father, or your family. Can't you understand I don't want to talk about those things? Not when all of them bring to mind the image of my mother's blood spilling across the kitchen floor. My father's blood caked into the grout."

I stop struggling in his grip and stare into his eyes. He's cleared the emotion from his face, presenting the mask he always did before... except now, I see something else in his eyes. Pain. So much pain he must be drowning in it.

I cup his cheeks and shake my head. "I need to talk about these things because they aren't settled. All of them are stacked up, creating this barrier between us. If you want me to give myself to you, we have to clear them out of the way. No matter how painful it is. Until then, I can't give you what you want from me."

His hands grip my hips, but I wiggle free and put a few steps between us.

As he narrows his eyes, I shake my head. "You said no to my deal, so I'll go back to our room now." I turn to the door to leave.

"Stop," his voice rings out in the room.

But I don't listen, increasing my pace to clear the threshold.

I don't get far before I hear the heavy thud of his steps on the hardwood as he gives chase.

13

NIC

"You can't get away from me," I call, not bothering to walk faster since there's nowhere in the house she'll be able to hide.

Her bare feet slap on the hardwood ahead of me before going silent, which means she either stopped or shifted over to the hallway with the runner. I turn the corner and spot the ends of her hair as she ducks into her old bedroom.

I brace my hands on the open doorway and peer into the darkened room. Once I moved her to mine, I had the staff clear this one out, so she had no option to return. All that's left inside is the bare furniture and heavy curtains across the windows.

"Princess? You can't hide from me. Come out now, and I'll make this easier on you."

I listen hard, focusing on any movement or sound. The bathroom door is closed, so I don't think she made it in there before I got to the door.

If she won't come out, I'll have to go in after her and show her exactly what happens when she defies me.

It takes seconds to find her hiding behind one of the curtains, her bare toes peeking out from the edge of the steel gray drapery. I tug back the curtain to find her staring up at me, her hands curled around the edge of the windowsill like it might anchor her.

"What do you think I should do to you, princess? You not only tried to manipulate me, but then you ran and didn't come out when I ordered. I think that deserves a punishment."

Her pulse pounds in the column of her neck, and she swallows heavily. "Punishment?"

I capture her neck in my hand and gently ease her toward me. "Just because you belong to me now doesn't mean you can act any way you please."

"What are you going to do?"

Unlike before, she doesn't look scared now, curious maybe, nervous even... "Unbuckle my belt," I order.

She locks our gazes for a heartbeat before reaching to my buckle and quickly completing the task, leaving the belt hanging from the loops.

"Take it off me."

Her heavy swallow is loud enough for me to hear as she slowly slides the leather from the loops of my pants.

"Good girl. Place it in my hand and then lay over the end of the bed."

Her eyes widen as she figures out my plan. But she doesn't hesitate as she steps around me to drape herself over the end of the bed. "You're behaving now, *stellina*. It makes me think you like this more than you let on."

My cock is straining at the waistband of my pants, looking at her like this. That fucking dress flowing over her curves, waiting for me to rip it off her.

I ease up behind her and drag her hips up so I can rub against them for a moment. It's not part of the punishment; it's just for me—a moment looking down as the dress billows around my pant legs.

She sucks in a breath and hides her face into the mattress.

"Are you ready, princess?"

Instead of answering, she eases her thighs apart slightly, squaring her feet on the floor.

"I'm not doing this to hurt you, just to teach you a lesson. So, we'll start with three blows. If you can manage that, then I'll forgive you." I add nothing about her not being able to handle it because I know even though this is her punishment, she wants it.

Her toes are curled into the floor, her breathing is ragged and strained. As is mine. I grip the belt tight in my palm and reach to the hem of her dress to drag it up around her hips.

"Fuck." The curse slips out before I can stop it. The little brat didn't wear any panties before she came to my office. She really thought she could walk in and seduce me.

I tuck the dress around her lower back to keep it out of the way.

There's no warning when I bring the leather down onto the softest part of her ass. At the strike, she lets out a soft hiss but then goes silent. It isn't a hard hit. We haven't done anything like this before. I don't know how much she can tolerate and how many makes her wet.

A pink line bisects her left ass cheek in a fat bar. Almost matching the color of her dress.

Holy hell, it looks good on her. I don't know if I'll make it to the third blow before I take her. My pulse is thundering in my ears.

"How are you feeling, princess?"

When she doesn't answer, I lean my hips into hers and chafe my hand over her pink skin. Her whimper belies the way she lifts her hips into mine to get the friction she wants.

"More?" I whisper and ease off her.

"Please," she says so softly I can barely hear her.

"Please, stop?" I prompt, knowing she doesn't want that, just as I know she's begging for more than my belt.

"No, again."

I smile down at her. Fucking hell, my princess is so perfect. "Say it again, and I'll give you everything you want and more. Beg me to punish you, and I'll fuck you until you come all over me."

Her ragged answer is everything I hope for. "Please, do it again."

Fuck yes, she does, and she deserves her reward afterward. I'm stunned by her. In awe of the way she's growing under my care, the way she's changing into the woman she is meant to become. My fucking princess will be my queen.

The next blow causes her to whimper, biting her lip afterward as if she tries to stifle it. The smack a loud crack in the silent room. A matching mark decorates her skin alongside the other. "Just fucking beautiful."

She's grinding her hips into the mattress, so I seize them to halt her movements. "No, princess. Your pain belongs to me, and so does your pleasure. Don't move."

I drop the belt to the floor with a clatter and work my fly open. She wiggles back toward me, and I groan as I wrap my hand around my cock.

I force myself to stop and take a deep breath. Then I step forward and run myself along the seam of her ass. "Where do you want me, princess? You took your punishment so beautifully. I'm in the mind to reward you. Do you want me in your ass or in your pussy?"

She doesn't answer, so I rub her raw skin, drawing her attention. "Say it, princess, or you can't have me, and I'll put you on your knees and fuck your pretty lips instead."

"Pu...Pussy," she stutters.

"Good girl. That wasn't so hard, was it? Next time, answer me when I ask you a question."

I dip myself down between her thighs. Fuck, she's so wet. I slide between her legs so easily. But that's not all I want. Before I ease both our aches, I want a taste of her.

I drop to my knees behind her and drag her ass into my face, spreading her open more as I spear my tongue into the moisture gathering between her thighs. So sweet and all for me.

She gasps and presses back into me, trying to give me better access— greedy little brat.

I lick her in long strokes as I wrap my fingers into her upper thighs to keep hold of her. She's squirming against me, against the bed, writhing for more.

When I can't wait any longer, I stand again, angling her hips to make it easier for me to slip inside her. Our height difference makes this position tricky, but she's so light I can lift her easily to make sure we fit together perfectly.

I nudge her entrance, carefully sliding inside her, one inch at a time. But she isn't as patient as I am, easing toward me as I glide forward. "You're not in charge here, princess. Stay still so I can fuck you properly. When you wiggle and squirm, as hot as it fucking is, I can't keep the angles I want to make sure you're properly taken care of."

She doesn't speak but goes still in my hands. It seems like she's willing to listen to my orders when they benefit her. A queen indeed.

I angle her hips up, lifting her effortlessly so I can fit her back into me, sink all the way inside her. When she shifts again, I pause, letting her get used to the feel of me filling her up. Sex is new to her, and she can't stretch around me easily yet. Her cunt is a tight grip around my cock, making it difficult to concentrate.

Carefully, I ease out of her until just the tip of me is inside her. I stare down at where our bodies join and enjoy the pink streaks from my belt in the view. Then I arch forward, pushing all the way inside again. She's stretching around me, this pass is wetter, her body taking me like it's made for me.

"Fuck, princess, you look so good wrapped around me," I whisper.

"Are you going to talk me to death or fuck me?" she says, her tone snippy.

I pause and smile down at her. The mouth on her, I should pull out and deny her an orgasm for that lip. Instead, I slap her ass right over the belt marks and enjoy the yip she gives me.

"Watch your mouth, or I won't let you come. And before you ask, don't worry. I'll make sure I do, but you won't until I give you permission."

To make sure she received my message, I smack her other ass cheek, enjoying the way she clenches around me as her muscles seize under the pain. "Glad we're on the same page now."

I reposition my hands again and start using her body to create a smooth tempo. Each stroke of her sheath around me is sheer bliss. I could stay here forever. But then I look up at her face. Her eyes are squeezed shut, her forehead bunches, her fingers digging into the texture of the mattress. My princess needs to come, and soon. She's on edge with the need for it. It's the only thing that would have made her mouth off to me.

"I'll take care of you," I tell her, moving faster, slamming her body back into mine as I press forward. She groans, and with each pass, her face smooths out under the pleasure.

The image of my cum running down her thighs amps my arousal higher. Then, inexplicably, the feel of her against me as I fuck her, my hand cradling her swollen belly, my child growing inside her.

I bark out a curse and pull out of her. She whimpers as her feet hit the floor again. But I don't have any intention of stopping. I lift her and toss her up onto the mattress, shove my pants and shoes off, then climb up behind her on the bed.

Once I've got myself behind her. I turn her on her side, lift her thigh bent at the knee, and lay it over mine, so I can slip inside her from behind again.

She doesn't comment on the change of the position, but that image sent my balls up and shoved me so close to orgasm. The thought of her carrying my baby inside her is too much to resist.

I angle my hips to get inside her, then bring my hand between her thighs to rub her clit while I fuck her hard and fast. Her hair fans across my chest as she rocks between my cock and my fingers, seeking her orgasm.

The second she finds it, the pulse of her body spurs my own. I drop my hand to her hips and use her body, fucking into her, relentless until I finally come with a shout against her hair. Once I can feel my fingers again, I ease my hold on her and hug her to my chest.

"What was that?" she asks.

I kiss her hair and pull her entire body flush to mine. "What do you mean?"

"You were behind me, and then you just changed positions suddenly."

I tilt her chin so I can look into her eyes. "Are you actually complaining right now?"

She shakes her head. "No, of course not. It was just strange."

"Don't worry about it." I drag the top of her dress down so I can cup her breast in my hand. It's full, and her nipple is tipped and hard. Will they swell when she gets pregnant?

It amazes me how fast I latch onto this idea of her carrying my child. Of her swollen and round with my baby. But then, on its heels, I know there's one more step in between before it can become a reality. Before she can grow my child in her womb, she needs to become my wife.

I run my lips down her cheek and take her mouth in a heated kiss. Delving my tongue between her lips to taste all of her. She moans, and I break away from her mouth and continue running my lips down her jawline to her neck. I deliver a little nibble at the column there and enjoy the way she wiggles away from me.

"No, princess. No matter how far you run, I'll always be able to find you. You'll never escape me."

She relaxes into me. "You know you sound like a creeper when you talk like that."

I spank her ass again, and I laugh as she shifts away, trying to outrun the pain that's already blooming.

"A creeper, really?"

She rolls in my arms, her dress bunching around our legs. "Hey, you're the one giving me these openings."

I shake my head. "When did you get so lippy? Do you need another punishment already?"

She huffs against my lips. "No, I don't think I could handle another one. I'll behave."

I bring our hips together and enjoy the way she closes her eyes as she relaxes into me again. "I doubt you'll ever behave, but as long as you remember you're mine, that's all I need. The rest, you'll learn."

14

CELIA

I feel different today. It's not just the ebbing soreness from our escapades in the hallway. But something else. A lightness in my chest that is new.

We haven't settled anything between us because neither of us has brought up the topics he refuses to talk about. And I know I should push for it, but I fear pushing him too far.

I close my eyes and let out a long exhale. If I have to admit it, I don't want to lose this. I don't think he'll go back to treating me the way he did before, but I also love the way he touches me. And I love the way he looks at me, like I'm the only woman in the entire world.

Today he's allowed me in the library alone. The balcony doors are open, and I'm standing at the entrance, letting the breeze wash over me. The air is warm and carries the scent of flowers, although I haven't seen any from my limited view of the property.

My mind automatically goes back to the last time I was here, and Nic took me on the grass. Claiming me, as he continues to do, every time we have sex.

That's something else I love about his treatment of me. He is fearless; if he wants something, he takes it. And while that hasn't always worked out in my favor, it does now when he's determined to give me more pleasure than I've ever felt in my entire life.

But it isn't just pleasure. He also touches me with a reverence that leaves me in awe.

I walk back into his office and glance at the desk, remembering the time he used my body. It was our first sexual encounter, and I hated him then. It seems like forever ago, even though only a few weeks have passed.

Memories of his body behind mine flood my head, his dick tucked between my thighs. The entire affair had been visceral, messy, almost dehumanizing... but it wasn't. At least not looking back at it.

It seems my body and my brain have gone on a strike together, and all because the big brute tweaked some nerve endings in a pleasurable way. He might be as insane as he is gorgeous, but there's no way I'm going to fall for him.

The door to the library opens behind me, and I glance toward it. Soo walks in. I guess it's a casual day for him since he's wearing a pair of slacks and a white button down. The uniform for him and Nic, it seems.

I give him a nod, which he returns.

When he doesn't leave, I wait for him to say something, but the silence stretches long and loud.

"Did you need something?"

He faces the bookshelves and makes a show of inspecting the spines. It hasn't escaped my notice that this house has a vast library, and I've seen none of the men who live here actually reading.

"I know you're not here to look for a book. Did Nic send you in here to babysit me?"

Soo glances over his shoulder at me. "Babysit? Wow. You sure have a way with words. And a way of degrading my position here."

I turn all the way around so I can actually face him. Especially if we're going to do one of these verbal sparring matches. "Well, I'm glad you're here. I actually wanted to ask you something."

He shoves his hands into his pockets and faces me. Now I have his full attention.

"I want to know if Nic seems different to you."

"How do you mean?"

I try to play things casually. But I'm well aware I'm a shitty liar, and both he and Nic are experts at detecting them. "I just mean, does he seem different to you? Not just the way he's acting toward me, but just different?"

Soo studies me now, cocking his head in the same way Nic does when he is trying to figure me out. "If I thought Nic was acting differently, and I'm not saying I do, I wouldn't be discussing it with you."

"Not even if I can make him happier than he is now?"

He scoffs. "And what makes you think he's happy? You may be in his bed, and he may treat you differently, but there are too many things he needs to finish before he might describe himself as happy."

To be fair, happy probably wasn't the right word to use in the situation. "I just mean maybe there's something I can do to help make his life easier."

Even I think that is a terrible excuse for my questioning. And I don't doubt for a second he can see right through me.

I throw up my hands and shake my head. "I'm sorry. I just don't know what to think. He's acting so differently than from how he acted before, and I'm just worried, I guess, that he's going to stop."

He doesn't acknowledge my statement or apology. Instead, he drags a book from the shelf and gives me a withering look. "Before I leave, is there anything you need?"

It's one of those questions that he really doesn't want answered. No doubt Nic sent him in here to check on me, and he's just being thorough so he can report back that I'm safe and sound.

Since he's being a dick, I guess I'll be one right back. "Well, while we're talking, maybe I can convince you to take me to see Lucas."

Surprise flickers across his face before he can snatch it back. It feels like a victory until he opens his mouth. "We both know that I'm not taking you anywhere near Lucas."

"But Nic trusts you. He knows you would keep me safe."

"Sure, but that doesn't mean he won't murder me for taking you there against his wishes. Wishes he's made quite clear to me, the rest of the staff, and Lucas himself. You are not to go near him."

We both know if anyone is safe from murder in this room, it's him. But I don't point that out. I'm tired of both him and Nic treating me like a glass doll balancing on a precipice. "If you won't take me to see him, will you at least let me write him a letter and deliver it?"

Again, he shakes his head. "Not going to happen. As I said, Nic would kill me, and then he would tie you to his bed until he's had his fill of you. And that would be merely the start of your punishment."

It disturbs me to hear him referencing anything to do with Nic and my sex life. I rack my brain, trying to think of something to say that might convince him. All the while, he's watching me, waiting to see what I'll do next. It makes me feel a bit like a bug in a jar.

Even as I switch tactics, I know I will regret it. "Who knew Nic has such a tight leash on you? I thought you were his best friend, not his underling."

Soo tosses his book on the nearest side table and stalks across the room toward me. It doesn't occur to me I should be afraid. Of everyone in this house, he's been the kindest to me from the beginning. But there isn't a sliver of that kindness in his gaze now.

"Listen, you may play these games of dominance and submission with Nic, but I am a different type of monster. I guarantee if your punishment were in my hands, you wouldn't enjoy yourself nearly as much."

Before I can say anything or even expel the outrage building up inside me, he grabs his book again, walks out the door, and slams it behind him.

It doesn't take long for Nic to come find me in the library. I wait for some kind of censure for how I talked to Soo, but it doesn't come. Which makes me wonder if Soo even told him what I asked or how I acted.

When he holds his hand out to me, I stare at it a heartbeat too long.

"What's wrong?" he asks.

I quickly shake my head and clasp my hand in his. "Nothing, I just wasn't sure what you wanted from me."

He leads me out of the house into a waiting car, and I don't even ask about our destination. I'm just so excited to get out.

"Soo suggested you might be going a little stir crazy, and that you wanted some new scenery."

A hot wash of shame hits my cheeks, and I turn my face to stare out the window so he doesn't see. I was an asshole to Soo, and he still showed me kindness.

The drive only takes a couple of minutes. We stop next to a sports field lined with small trees. I stare out at the greenery, and I realize I've been here before. Years ago.

"Where are we?"

"Just a little park near my house."

He helps me out of the vehicle and tucks my hand in his as I stare around. The memory hits me in a flash—me as a child. I don't know how old, and the boy who was my best friend, playing here. There used to be a swing set and a sandbox to one side of the field, but it looks like they were removed. It's been so long since I thought about that boy. I face Nic now and stare up into his eyes. "It's strange that we're here. I've been here before. Actually, this is where I got my scar."

He nudges my hair out of my face and traces the line of it down my cheek with his thumb. "How did it happen?"

I point toward the empty field, the memory rising from the recesses of my mind. "We were young, my friend and I. We were playing on one of those dome jungle gym things. Some idiot came over and tried to start a fight with him. They grappled, and I tried to protect him, but he accidentally caught me in the face with his pocketknife. He'd stolen it from his father."

I can taste the heat in the air that day. It was so hot a permanent shimmer rose over the asphalt of the parking lots. We'd been running wild since lunch, dirt and peanut butter smeared on our cheeks.

A wave of nausea washes over me, threatening to drag me into the memory. That was the last day I saw the boy I thought I would one day marry. His family disappeared soon after.

His thumbs are still gentle as he rubs over the scar and curls up around my eyelid. I close my eyes and fall into the sensation of his touch. It's soft and assertive. There's never any question with him. When he wants to touch me, he touches me, and he does it with conviction.

"This friend, who is he?" There's an odd note in his tone.

Along with the memories, an old, aching grief stirs. That summer was the last time I saw him. Now, I barely even think about him, and it makes me feel all the worse.

"His father and mine were friends. We used to do everything together, but then one day, after his parents died, he disappeared. I guess I assumed they had shipped him off to live with some distant relative, but by the way the servants talked about the incident, I think he was killed with them, and they just didn't want to tell me."

His gaze is filled with something I can't name. Not grief, but something warmer, softer, more forgiving. "What else did you two do together?"

My smile rises without thought as I dredge up old memories from the depths of my mind. "Well, we used to camp in the yard. His younger brother always wanted to come and play with us, but my friend didn't want him to because he got scared in the dark and would cry half the night until his mom picked him up. We also explored the little tunnel system under his old mansion. They were pretty cool. Built for bootleggers or something like that, a long time ago."

"You look happy when you speak of him."

I nod. "I feel bad for not thinking about him more, but yes, it makes me happy to remember the times we shared, but also sad to think about how he's not in my life anymore. When I got older and started battling with my father over marriage prospects and party planning, he would have understood the kind of life I wanted to lead and married me, so I could go to college and do what I wanted instead of becoming a trophy wife and a dowry for his family."

"He sounds like he would have been an honorable man. Why did you think he would have married you?"

A laugh pops out of me even as tears well in my eyes. "Because he asked me once when we were younger. Saying once we got married, we'd be the most powerful house in the six families. He'd become the ruler of them all, and I'd be his queen. But he used one of those bread ties. It was orange, and he fashioned it into an engagement ring for me. I still have it in a shoebox under my bed at home. Well, if my mother didn't throw out all my possessions by now."

His eyes are bright and warm as he scans my features. I lean into his touch, letting his palm cup around my cheek. It feels so good when he touches me like this. There's conviction, but also an underlying layer of tenderness he'd never displayed until after he rescued me from Lucas's house.

I blink my eyes open. And I try to gather up the courage I need to say what I want to know. Because it's killing me not to have the answers I want.

As if he can read my mind, he smiles. "Whatever you need to say, just say it."

"Why are things so different between us?" I blurt out.

"Is that why you were interrogating Soo? What all this anxiety and fear on your face is about?"

I nod. In the grand scheme of things, it doesn't matter. He's said many times that he will not let me leave.

He opens his mouth to answer, but then a white and blue soccer ball streaks by us and stops a few feet away.

I hadn't even noticed the small group of college-age guys playing nearby. One man runs over to retrieve the ball, and while he does, he gives me one of those arrogant once-overs, scanning me from head to toe.

Nic stiffens beside me, his hands stilling on my skin. I remember how he acted in the restaurant when the waiter accidentally touched me. My eyes catch on his, and the flickering of rage in them tells me I need to get him away from this man before he murders him and fucks me in a puddle of his blood just to prove a point.

15

NIC

*S*he tugs on my hands and tries to lead me away, but I lock my gaze on the fucking kid who thinks he can look at my princess.

"Can I help you?" I ask him with deadly calm.

He's not smart enough to realize he's in trouble now. Because if she weren't right here holding my hands, I'd already be on him, punching in his face, ripping out his eyes for looking at what's mine.

The kid shakes his head, realization slowly leaking into his features. "Nah, man, I'm good, just getting my ball."

"Then get your fucking ball and walk away. Don't look at her again, and tell your friends to keep their eyes on your game, or you'll all regret it."

He scoffs. "Whatever, man." He tosses the ball in the air toward his friends and bounds away.

I'm coiled tight with rage, ready to go after him, teach him a lesson in respect.

Celia grips my cheeks and drags my focus to her. "Look at me, Nic. Please, look at me now." Her voice is frantic.

I focus on her pretty face, anger still coursing through me. "I'm looking at you. Keep talking to me."

She releases a tiny sigh of relief to have reached me. "Don't think about those dumb guys. It's a habit to look at a woman more than anything."

I trap her hands under mine. "Don't talk about that, or I'll go over there and kill them all."

Her forehead bunches as she studies me. "You'd kill them for looking at me. Don't you think that's sort of messy?"

"Doesn't matter. I protect what's mine. I keep what's mine, and as I said..."

"I belong to you, yes, you've mentioned that a time or two."

Something eases in my shoulders. "I'm glad you were listening."

As I relax, so does she, but she doesn't know how close to the edge I still am. "Let's go back to the car."

She nods, tucking my hand into hers and leading me toward the vehicle like she thinks I might make a break for it and go feral on the college kids.

I glance over my shoulder to find they've moved down the field away from us. The kid is smarter than he looks.

Gently, I help her into the vehicle and climb in after her, closing the door. She moves to her side, but I drag her back to mine, tucking her under my arm. "No, let me hold you, reassure myself with your presence."

She lays her hand on my chest, snuggling into the curve of my arm. "Did you go to college?"

I shake my head. "No, there was no need. I was building an empire. Everything I've learned, I learned on the streets. There isn't exactly a degree program for street justice and commerce."

"But there has to be something you wanted to do before you created your... empire." Her tone says she wants to use a different noun, but I let it go.

"No, when our parents were killed, there wasn't any time to consider what we wanted. For a long time, our lives were only about survival. And after we finally established our territory, our goal became growth, maintaining, and vengeance." It's the reason I keep my secrets to myself. To know me is a burden more than a gift.

She nods against me, dropping her gaze. There's no need to bring up the facts again and ruin the moment, and I'm thankful she doesn't want to start a fight right now. Not when I'm primed to do damage. I'd never hurt her like that, but I might say something she doesn't want to hear and won't forget easily.

I look at her from this angle. Fuck, she's beautiful. The soft slope of her nose leads down to full plush lips I love to look at. One day, I'm going to buy her every shade of fuck me red lipstick just to watch her put them on.

One day, like we have a future, an actual life. The idea comforts me, easing my shoulders down from my ears further.

"Do you want children?" The question slips out without me thinking about how she might take it first. But she doesn't act like it's strange.

She nods at me. "Yeah, of course. I want a huge family, lots of kids running around. I love babies. They smell so good."

"And do you plan on staying home with all these children, taking care of them?"

Her smile is bright as she lifts her face to look at me. "Yes, of course. While I used to study psychology as a hobby and wanted to go to school for it, I always knew that eventually, I'd want to raise a family. I've never had a real one. My sister was the closest thing to familial love I've ever gotten. I want to have babies and give them all the love I didn't get when I was a child. To love them and teach them how to be kind and caring people."

I tilt her chin to kiss her lips. "I think you'll be an incredible mother."

Her pink flush warms something in my chest. "Thank you."

I signal the driver to take us back to the house. Since her punishment, the vision of her swollen with my child has been stuck in my mind. I can't get enough of her. And right now, I want to lie between her spread thighs and come inside her until she's full of my seed.

When we reach the house, Soo is lurking in the foyer.

I kiss her cheek and whisper in her ear. "Go up to the room and get naked. Then lay down on the bed and wait for me."

If arguing enters her mind, she doesn't show it. To my amazement, she nods at Soo and heads up to our bedroom.

"I tried to call you," Soo says. "Sorry to interrupt your afternoon plans, but we need to think about the next steps."

I sigh. "You're right. But there's something I need to do first, or I won't be able to focus on it."

"What's that?"

I glance up at the hallway leading to our bedroom. "I need to make sure Celia can't slip away from me again, no matter what happens."

"You think she'll try to run?"

I don't anymore, but it doesn't mean I'll take the risk with her. "No, but I want to make sure she doesn't have the option. I need to make sure."

He nods. "Okay. I'll start on my own while you handle your business. Let me know if you need anything."

Any other man, it might have been a taunt, but I trust Soo completely, more than anyone in my life. Ever since the day we were sixteen, staring down the barrels of another gang's guns. Neither of us had a reason to trust, but somehow, when we looked at each other, we agreed. We'd get out of it together. And we did.

I clap him on the shoulder, my focus shifting to my princess lying naked in our bed.

I race up the stairs and down the hall. When I open the door, I breathe out a sigh. And damn, I should say a prayer of thanks.

She's completely nude, stretched out flat on top of the made bed.

"I love it when you follow directions so prettily," I say, already stripping clothes as I cross to the side of the bed.

She scowls up at me but doesn't comment. No doubt remembering how much I enjoy punishing her when she lets her smart mouth run free.

I finish undressing and crawl up on the bed. She spreads her thighs open for me, her pussy already pink and gleaming. "Did you touch yourself while you waited?"

Her eyes go round, and after a second of hesitation, she nods once.

I run my hands up her thighs and smile down at her. "Naughty princess. I think you want me inside you right now. Say please."

"Please," she whispers.

I anchor my weight over her. My cock is already rock hard, and I love the way it looks pressed against her skin.

Carefully, I ease into her, watching as my body disappears into the cradle of hers. She sighs as every inch sinks into her warm heat. When I'm fully seated, she wraps her hands up to cup the back of my head. I lower my chest to hers slightly, still maintaining most of my weight on my forearms.

Then I grind my hips forward and ease out. Letting my cock brush over her sensitive bud to give her the friction she needs.

"Did you come when you touched yourself?" I ask, meeting her eyes as I fuck her.

"No," she breathes.

"Good girl. You remembered; your pleasure is mine."

I increase my pace, her body clenching around me with each arch of my hips. She feels so good underneath me.

Soon my body is slamming into hers as she thrashes her head and claws at my skin. I love the way her entire body shows her enjoyment. All too soon, she's coming, her pussy clenching as she gasps and pants underneath me. When she's finished coming, I stop moving and stare down at her sleepy smile.

"Marry me."

Her eyes pop open. "What?"

"Marry me, *stellina*. I want you to be my wife."

Her mouth bobs open and closed as she seeks something to say. I arch my hips forward, and she squeezes her eyes closed. I'm so close to coming, and I want to hear her say yes as I do, but I can't wait.

I push up to gain a different angle and slam into her a few more times, loving how her orgasm only adds to the slick slide of me into her body. I come with her name on my lips, and my forehead pressed into hers.

When I open my eyes, she is staring at me, searching my face, my gaze, everything. "Was that a serious question, or were you just messing with me?"

I shake my head. "I'm a monster, *stellina*, but I'm not that kind of cruel. I want to marry you. Say yes."

"I don't know if I can."

Still semi-hard, I ease into her a little bit. "If you marry me, I'll give you everything. I'll give you pleasure, money, jewels, houses, cars, you name it, and it'll be yours."

Her forehead scrunches in that cute little way I love when she's thinking too hard. "Are you trying to bribe me into saying yes?"

"I'd prefer not to, but let me remind you, I'll do anything to get what I want, and I want you."

She shoves at my chest, but I don't leave the warm, slick clasp of her body. "Marrying me won't mean I've given you my heart, especially if it's done with coercion."

"I'm confident I can earn your heart in time. If you can't say yes, at least tell me why."

She takes a second to answer, but when she does, she meets my gaze solidly. "I don't know what it means. Do you want to marry me because I'm some kind of conquest or because you care? And if I do marry you, and then you try to exact your revenge, I don't know if I'll be able to forgive you for it. Then where does that leave us?"

I asked for honesty. It doesn't mean every word isn't a sharp stab to my chest. "What can I do to prove I want you?"

She laughs, her body tightening around me. "I think you being inside me right now at least proves you want me. Lust has never been an issue with us, but marriage, love, isn't the same thing, is it?"

Is love what I'm offering? I brush her hair away from her face. "I'll be honest. I'm not sure if I'm capable of love. But I know about commitment, loyalty, safety. These things I can give you."

She narrows her eyes at me as if considering. I kiss her, knowing I can't handle whatever else she might say to me. "Let me prove to you that your pleasure and your comfort will come first to me."

I slide down her body and widen her thighs. My cum is dripping out of her cunt, and it makes a possessive ache spear my chest, chasing away her doubts. I'm the only man who's been inside her, and I'll be the only man she has.

I lean down and lick her clit, tugging the swollen nub between my lips. She arches up and spears her fingers into my hair.

"Oh, my god," she whispers.

I suck on her clit gently until she's rocking up toward my face in time with each drag of her flesh between my lips.

Then I lap at her flesh, enjoying the way she squirms, trying to get more from me, demanding more, even as she writhes in my grip.

I lift my head, and she drops her knees and groans in frustration. "This is what you have to look forward to if you say yes. I'll make you come every single night we're together."

"Solid argument," she whispers, thrusting her hips up toward me.

I dip my head back down and fuck her with my tongue until she comes again, groaning and gripping my head.

When she eases down, I climb back up her body and settle in beside her on the bed. Gently, I tuck her against my side and run my hand down her front to ease my fingers over her belly.

"Why do you want to marry me?" she asks after a while.

I can lie, but right now, I don't want to, not to her. "Because once I lost my parents, it was like I lost my name, too. I had nothing. The moment I made myself a Diavolo, I vowed my son will never face that feeling. I'll be married to his mother, and he will have my name. He'll be a Diavolo and have respect just for that."

"What if your child is a girl?"

I stare down at her and smile. "Then she'll have my name, and the city will quake when she comes into her power. You might already know this, but women are more ruthless than men in defense of their territories."

She smiles, her eyes bright as she looks up at me. When she wraps her hand up around my neck and kisses me, I let her take the lead, take what she wants from me.

Now I just need to make her believe I can give her everything, and as my wife and my queen, she'll have more power than she's ever known.

16

CELIA

The next morning, Nic is sitting on the end of the bed, a black dress draped across his already clothed lap. I shove the covers out of the way so I can see him better. "Are you all right?"

He drags his gaze to mine as if he were far away. "Of course, get dressed, and I'll have Sarah bring you some breakfast. I wanted to give you this. I have to go finish a couple of things before we leave."

He stands and lays the dress on the bed. But I can't shake the feeling that something is wrong.

As he walks out, I call out to snag his attention. "Where are we going?"

With his hand on the door, his body already partially in the hallway, he stops. "It's a surprise. Get dressed, and you'll see soon enough." I can't see his face as he speaks since it's hidden behind the heavy wooden door, but there's something in his voice I can't pinpoint.

When he leaves, it's as if all the air in the room goes with him. And it's not because there's one huge question hovering between us. Or maybe it is.

Nic asked me to marry him last night. It still seems surreal. Like he's going to walk back in the bedroom and tell me it's all a joke or a cruel trick he used to force my guard down.

And the worst part, I'm not sure I don't want it all to be a joke. Maybe he can see it in my eyes, and that's why he looked so... defeated just now.

I clean up and dress quickly. By the time I leave the bathroom, a breakfast tray is sitting on the bed. I barely have a few moments to scarf down a couple of bites of toast before Nic returns, his immaculate suit in place, and his jaw tense.

"Are you going to tell me where we're headed?"

He cups my cheeks in his hands and drags me up to his mouth. Obviously, meeting me halfway since the height between us is all in his favor. When he pulls away, I'm breathless, and he says, "Where's the fun in that?"

My worry turns into excitement. I'm smiling as I snag the rest of the toast, slip my feet into some black ballet flats, and let Nic lead me out to the car. For him, this dress is practically matronly. I wonder when he picked it out. Everything up till now has been slightly sexy, sometimes daring.

When we pull up outside a familiar apartment, I take a moment to memorize the lines of it in the light of day. Now the demure clothing makes sense. "Why didn't you tell me we were coming?"

The entire car ride has been tense, and he hasn't touched me since he helped me into the vehicle. Something that's strange for him. Whenever we are in the same room, he always has his hands on me. If not on my skin, in my hair, or around the back of my neck.

"I wanted it to be a surprise."

I try to smile to let him know how much I appreciate this. And even more, I try not to over-analyze it because all I can wonder is why now? And did he do this to ensure I say yes to his proposal? Last night, he promised to let me make the choice on my own. However, I never mentioned enticement.

I stare up at the building. And showing me trust, finally, definitely entices me. He comes around and helps me out of the car.

We get to the door, and Lucas answers after one knock. "What do you want?"

Nic clears his throat, and I can't see him from where he's positioned behind me, but Lucas's face makes me think he doesn't appreciate the attitude.

Instead of arguing, he steps away from the door to let us inside. He's cleaned up the mess from the tussle between him and Nic.

Once we sit on the couches, Lucas throws himself in a chair and glares, dragging his eyes between us to make sure it registers with both of us.

I turn to face Nic and take his hands in mine. "Can I have a minute alone with Lucas?"

He grits his teeth, tightening his palm around mine. "Absolutely not."

"He won't hurt me. And I just want to talk to him, and I don't think he's going to say anything in front of you."

"He will if I beat him into it."

I cup his cheek in my palm, forcing him to look at me head on. "I understand why you brought me here. You want me to know, truly know, things are different now. However, you have to know when to ease up."

"I can't leave you alone with another man."

I wave at Lucas. "He's not going to touch me, either. How about you go into the bedroom and stay there until I call you out? At the very least, give me the illusion of privacy."

He takes a long time to decide, staring around the room, pinning Lucas with a death glare. Finally, he stands, buttons his suit jacket, and heads back into the bedroom. Before he closes the door, he calls out. "You only have a few minutes. When I come back out, the meeting is over."

The room feels bigger without his demanding presence at my side. Lucas clears his throat pointedly but doesn't say anything.

"Sorry, he's being weird. We're trying to decide something."

"Looks like you're trying to decide something. I know my brother. He's already made his choice."

I'm not touching that one. He looks much better since the night Nic found me. I'm reminded of the way he looked that night when I left.

"Did you see a doctor for your ribs?"

He crosses his arms over his chest and narrows his eyes. "Is that why you're here, so you can ask me about my health? Next time call and save us both the time."

Damnit. He's so much like his brother. So fucking hardheaded. However, Nic has some temperance to his stubbornness, whereas

Lucas would argue the sky is green just because someone else insists it's blue.

"You know, I didn't come here to talk about your numerous issues. I'm here because I have some questions I think you can answer." I force myself to breathe after I get all the words out.

Lucas takes so much time to answer. I think he's about to fling more profanity and waste the time I have left. But he nods once, giving me permission.

My chest loosens, and I nod heavily. "Tell me about your childhood."

"Pass."

I jerk back from the vehemence in his tone. "You don't want to talk about you two as kids at all?"

"Nope. And if that's your entire line of questioning, you should just leave now."

I don't bother trying to hide my disappointment. "Well, can you tell me more about what you know about my father and my sister?"

This gets his attention. He drops his boots from the edge of the coffee table to thump on the floor. "Are you finally understanding what kind of man your father is?"

"I'm not saying anything. I only asked you a question. What do you know about it? How do you know about it?"

A cruel smile twists his lips, and something tells me he is enjoying this. Maybe not my pain directly, but dismantling any fantasy I might harbor involving my father. "Soo, as you are well aware by now, keeps tabs on everyone. Their movements, their digital footprint, all of it. He was watching your father that night, and worse, when the family your sister was about to marry requested the proof of her demise to maintain their continued support, he sent a video from his cell phone. The same cell phone Soo had cloned. Now, Soo has the video and every other naughty thing your father has done."

He whips out his cell phone, turns it to face me, and hits the play button. "I asked him to forward me this when I saw Nic caught you."

He keeps talking, but the sound seems to dampen to a fuzzy ringing that takes over as I blink and try to force myself under control. I hadn't wanted to hear what they had to say about him, my own blood, and yet, proof? I'm watching it, but I can't see it through the haze over my vision. I want to deny the hand holding the gun isn't my father's, but there's his signet ring, the one he never removes.

"Enough," a hard voice orders from far away.

A cool hand touches my cheek, and like I'm swimming up through heavy rapids, I turn to face the person standing there touching me. Nic. Of course.

He's shouting at Lucas, cursing, and the phone goes flying across the room. I catch his hands and shake my head, my breathing shallow and my head dizzy.

My sister.

"Celia," Nic says, louder this time.

I shake myself, and the room comes rushing back around us in overwhelmingly bright focus. "No, I'm here."

Both men are watching me closely now, as if they are waiting for me to tip off the couch and shatter onto the floor.

"We're leaving," Nic announces, rising from his crouch.

I tear my hand from his. "We aren't finished here. I have more to ask him. A few more minutes, please?"

He paces around the space like a wild animal, then stops, staring down at me. "I'll be outside the door. You have two minutes. Hurry."

After he walks out, I focus on Lucas again. "Well, since we're under a time crunch..."

Lucas is staring at the apartment door Nic just left from. "He seems different."

There's no way he can know, and I'll never admit it, but I'm grateful for the change of topic. My sister's death at the hands of our father is something I need to consider on my own. Not colored by his own views.

"How so?"

"He's had women, of course. But in all the years I've witnessed his personal life, I've never seen him how he is with you."

My mind immediately hops to the negative, assuming he means things are different with me because of who I am or how we came together. "What does that mean?"

As if he can see inside my head, he rolls his eyes. "With his other women, it was sex, and that's it. He never troubled himself with their comfort or safety. Once they left his sight, they were always on their own."

The news shoots a wave of relief through me, and yet, I feel like I'm surrendering by wanting him like I do, by needing him. "Well, that's interesting."

He snorts, like he knows exactly what I'm struggling with. Thankfully, he doesn't drag it into the light and make me face it.

"I better go before he comes in here and carries me out." I stand and face him. "I don't know where we stand, but if we're family, then I want to have a relationship with you. If you think you can handle having one with me. And know, I'm going to make this right."

His mouth drops open. Before he has the chance to run away, I reach up and hug him. As quickly as I wrap my arms around him, I turn away and head out the door.

Nic is standing next to it, leaning on the drywall. "Are you okay?"

I nod. "I'm ready to go. Thank you for bringing me here."

For a second, he looks like he wants to argue with me, but then he changes his mind and tugs me to his side. "I'm sorry he was so crude about your sister. While I also told you the truth, I know it's different facing the proof of something."

He walks me to the elevator and leads me to the car. When we pull away, he shifts to drag me into his lap. "Let me hold you."

"Why?" While our relationship has changed, the intimacy between us still leans heavily toward sex—except for his constant need to touch me.

"Because I want to, and because you want me to, even if you won't admit it out loud. That's okay. You don't have to admit it. Just sit here, shut up, and let me do it."

I tuck my head into his chest and let out a long exhale. Did my mother know my father killed my sister? How could she? There is very little she notices beyond the neck of a liquor bottle. Hell, she hadn't even helped at my sister's wake.

A wave of nausea rolls over me, and I clamp my hand over my mouth. We had a wake and a funeral for her. My father gave a eulogy beside her grave.

Nic massages the base of my neck until the nausea slows. But in its wake, something sharper takes shape in my gut, filling me up. It went so far beyond the paltry urge for revenge I'd harbored toward Nic when we first met. This need for vengeance feels like it can consume me if it's not satisfied.

"Are you okay?"

"Yes, but we need to talk about last night and what you offered me."

He shifts so I can meet his eyes. "Now? You want to talk about it right now?"

I nod. "You made me an offer. I told you I'd consider, and when I was ready to give you an answer, I would."

He grinds his teeth and tugs my hips into him. "Any decision you make right now is made in grief."

I keep my face neutral, force him to see I'm serious and that I'm making the choice willingly. "Does that mean you don't want to hear my answer or my conditions?"

It takes time for him to answer me. No doubt he fought some sort of inner struggle over it. But then he says, "Tell me."

I wrap my hands around his neck and arch up to press my forehead into his. "I'll marry you, but under one condition. It's non-negotiable."

His hands tighten on my hips, and I feel him growing hard between my thighs. "Tell me, *stellina*. It's not nice to tease a man."

"I'll be your wife if, and only if, when it comes time to kill my father, it's my finger on the trigger, and my eyes are the last ones he sees."

17

NIC

Only a few days have passed since I asked Celia to be my wife, and any minute now, she's going to walk into my office and tell me she's changed her mind. I catch myself every few minutes, halting my pacing to stare at the door. Simply to make sure she's not standing on the other side, bolstering her courage to reject me.

I have confined myself to my office, as every single person I encounter today seems to try to get in my way. After Sarah refused to make lunch for me, Soo suggested I prepare for the ceremony and then hide out in my office until it's time.

The result is I've not seen Celia since we woke up this morning, which has set me on edge. I'm not the kind of man who needs reassurance, and yet, I long to hear her voice in my ear, confirming she's mine. Hell, earlier, I even thought about sending a staff member out to buy her a cell phone, so I could at the very least call her.

I spin away from the door for the tenth time in the last hour and stalk toward the fireplace. The pacing is the only thing keeping me from ripping off my tuxedo in favor of something less restrictive.

The lowball of brandy in my hand doesn't hurt either. But the fear, the lack of food, and alcohol create a toxic sludge in my gut that threatens to end the celebration before it starts.

The afternoon sunlight is beaming through the windows. We could've held the ceremony outside, but it's always hard to know if the weather will cooperate in this part of the state. There is more room in this house than I will ever be able to fill, so it is nothing to have the staff decorate an empty ballroom for the event.

A sharp knock on the office door sends my hands shaking. "Come in," I shout.

Soo pokes his head through the door and peers around the room until he spots me practically huddling in the farthest corner. "Are you okay?"

"What do you want?" I growl.

He closes the door behind him. "You asked me to come and find you once the room was prepared. The priest is already waiting, and I think Celia is almost ready."

That snaps through the haze. "Have you seen her?"

"No, she refuses to let anyone into her room."

I cross to the door in a couple of long strides. "Why? Does she need anything? Is she having regrets? Maybe she's afraid to call everything off for fear of me."

Soo claps me on the shoulder, takes the drink from my hand, and swishes the rest of it back. "Let's go look at the room, so you can stretch your legs and calm the fuck down."

I follow him to the main floor and off to a rarely used ballroom. Soo shoves the doors open with little fanfare. But the inside of the room jerks me to a halt at the threshold.

A long white carpet runs up the center of the room to reach a small stage. A collection of chairs is arranged on either side of the carpet. But only a few, as this is going to be a very private ceremony. The staff has somehow erected a trellis above the chairs and strung tiny white lights from the wooden supports. And on top of those: white lilies. The scent of them hangs heavy in the air, giving the room a magical touch.

"Do you think she'll like it?" I ask Soo.

He nods. "I think she'll love it. But there's one more thing you need to take care of before she's done getting ready."

As always, he's right. I've been putting it off out of fear that seeing my face will scare her into running.

Soo catches my arm before I can head back toward the stairs. "Are you sure you want to do this?"

I grab the railing and meet his eyes. "I've never been more sure of anything in my life."

He offers a smile. "I'm here for you, man, and I'm happy for you."

Before things can get out of hand in the emotion department, I sprint upstairs to our room and dig a long garment bag from the back of the closet. It takes me another two seconds to reach the room, and I knock softly.

"Go away," she shouts.

I smile, thinking about how much yelling at the staff I've been doing today, too. Does she have the same fears? That I'll change my mind and leave her standing at the altar alone? The idea soothes me. Easing the ache in the pit of my gut for the first time all day.

"I have a gift for you."

"Just leave it!"

Instead of waiting for permission, I grip the handle and shove the door open. She's sitting in her white lace lingerie on the edge of the bed, a glass of wine clutched in her hand. "What are you doing here? You're not supposed to be in here."

I lay the dress on the bed and cup her cheeks. "Are you okay? What's wrong?"

She shakes her head. "Nothing is wrong. For the first time in a long time, I feel like I'm making the best choice." Her eyes snag on the bag, and she waves her glass toward it. "What's that?"

"A gift," I say, and carefully lower the zipper to reveal the dress inside. While she thought she would wear something else, I'd ensured she has a dress fit for the princess she is.

"Wow," she breathes, running her fingers over the exposed lace. "I guess I better put it on since we're supposed to go downstairs soon."

She carefully peels the dress from the bag and heads into the bathroom, where her makeup artist is still packing up her kit. When she closes the door behind her, I smile. If she hadn't, and I'd caught sight of her in her lingerie, we'd both be late for our own wedding.

When she exits the bathroom, I think my heart stops. She is stunning. Of course, she is beautiful no matter what she's wearing, but right now, her body wrapped in white lace that hugs every inch of her, I can't even think about how lovely she looks.

"It's beautiful, thank you."

It takes me two tries to clear my throat. "There's jewelry to match. Let me help you put it on."

I open the blue velvet box and lift out an intricate diamond wreath necklace. She gasps as the cold metal fits around her neck. Once it's secure, I fish out the earrings and bracelet to give her.

She faces me again and smiles, wide and warm, and it's enough to melt the ice I've kept my heart encased in since my parents died. Fuck, she is worth it, though.

"Are you having second thoughts?" I blurt out.

Her eyes dash to mine. "What? No. Do I look like I am? I promise. We made a deal, and I intend to honor it. Besides..." She steps into me and runs her hands up my lapels. "You look so fucking good in a tuxedo. I can't wait to strip it off you later."

"Watch it, princess, or we'll never make it downstairs, and all this work will have been for nothing."

The makeup artist and hair stylists that were set up in the bathroom slip out the door quietly. But she only has eyes for me. "How about you? Any regrets?"

I lift her chin with my fingers, tilting her head so I can capture her mouth, but instead of kissing her, I nibble on her bottom lip. When I release her lip, I say, "No. I have none. However, I have to admit, I'm not a big enough man to let you go now, even if you asked me, even if you begged."

Her breathing is uneven, and I know she has to be wet underneath all that lace for me. It takes all the control I've learned over the years not to find out. "Well, it looks like we are both on the same page. Although, every time I turn around, it seems you've outdone yourself with the staff or the decorations. Everything is lovely. It's exactly what

I would have chosen for my wedding myself. And I'll be honest, not at all what I expected."

"What did you expect?"

She shrugs, the lace parting around the lush curve of her breasts to entice me with a glimpse. "I don't know. An empty room, you in a suit, Soo officiating the wedding maybe. I wasn't expecting you to want to make it beautiful for me."

I deserve that, by the way things have progressed for us, but I will make her fucking learn her care comes first to me. "You might not believe it, but I want to make you happy. And eventually, once we get through all of this, I think you will be."

Her eyes search mine. "Why, though? That's something I'm having trouble with."

I smirk and kiss her knuckles. "Because you belong to me. And I take care of what's mine."

A heavy pounding on the door tells me it's time. "I'll see you downstairs," I tell her and turn to go.

It takes everything in me not to look back. Watch her for signs she might have doubts. Because even if I see those signs, I won't be able to let her go.

Soo and I head down to the ballroom. Lucas is sitting in one of the chairs as I stride up the aisle. He hadn't wanted to be here today, but I know Celia would want him to be. He's still acting as if I don't exist and that I've somehow fucked up his entire plan, but soon he'll realize I saved his fucking life.

I glare at him with a warning before taking my place in front of the priest, a small elderly man who looks slightly bemused about this entire situation but is amenable to doing his job.

Soft strains of piano music rise out of the speakers built into the room. Soo, of course, cues the song when Celia arrives to walk down the aisle. When she appears in the doorway, a white bouquet in her hands, I freeze, unable to take my eyes off her.

I'd already seen her in this dress, but not in this room, in this context, and I can't stop watching her as she slowly walks up the aisle alone.

When she reaches me, I'm still dumbstruck, so she takes my hand in hers and shifts me around to face the priest.

At my request, he keeps the ceremony brief and to the basics. And when I slip a slim platinum band onto her left ring finger, it's as if I can breathe fully for the first time since we began the ceremony.

The priest is smiling at us both when he says, "You may kiss your bride."

I face Celia, but before I can lower my lips to hers, she has her hand wrapped around the back of my neck, dragging me to meet her. She tastes sweet, like the wine she'd been drinking in her room, no doubt, and her mouth is smooth and warm as I clutch her tighter to my chest.

I don't know how long we stay this way, kissing, feeling each other, but someone clears their throat loud enough that we finally break apart. The assembled give us a small round of applause, including the priest. All except Lucas, who is staring with his usual brooding intensity as if he's waiting for something to happen, which might actually be worth his time.

We walk back down the aisle toward the door, and when we reach the threshold, I swing her up into my arms.

She lets out a squeal and fumbles with her bouquet.

"Are you ready?" I ask, nibbling on the outer shell of her ear.

"Almost. I have to get out of this dress first... and these shoes. They look amazing but feel like they are trying to strangle my toes."

"All right, but hurry. I'll be waiting at the door." I don't particularly want to let her out of my sight, but I have to talk to Soo and my men one last time before I can leave. Setting her back on her feet, I lean down. I kiss my bride on her painted lips softly before I watch her walk toward the staircase.

My *stellina*.

My bride... until death do us part.

18

CELIA

I hate the fact that one of the first things I say as his wife is a lie, but I know he wouldn't have let me talk to Lucas. Especially not on my own again.

Instead of heading upstairs, I spin around and speed walk back to the other side of the house. I saw Lucas go out to the terrace, and I hope that's where he is now. My high heels click on the tile floor, somehow louder than before.

Stopping, I quickly slip them off to carry them the rest of the way. Wife or not, I don't think the guards would listen to me and not rat me out to Nic.

Pushing open the terrace door, I step outside and immediately spot Lucas at the edge of the garden. He turns to look at me as I approach and shakes his head, almost like he is disappointed.

"Don't you have a honeymoon to go on?" He pulls out a pack of cigarettes, flips it open, and places one between his lips.

"I do, but I didn't want to leave without talking to you. You've been ignoring me," I accuse. "You're not supposed to ignore the bride at a wedding, you know?"

Tucking the pack back into his pocket, he pulls out a lighter and lights up the cigarette. "It's not like I wanted to be here. Nic basically forced me to show up."

"I figured as much. I'm still glad you came, though."

"Whatever." He shrugs, blowing out a big cloud of smoke between us.

"I didn't know you smoke." I shouldn't be surprised. After seeing his body all beaten and bruised, it's clear he doesn't care much about his health.

"There is a lot about me you don't know."

"Maybe I want to know more."

"We talked about this. We're not friends, and we're not family. We might share some genetics, but I couldn't care less about you."

I wish his words wouldn't hurt. I wish I could just brush them off and move on, but something inside me is holding onto the idea that we could actually build a relationship.

"Look. I know what you said before, and believe me, at first, I didn't want to consider you family either, but things have changed. You might not see me as family, but you do Nic, and I did just marry him."

"Why did you?" He takes another drag of his cigarette, letting the question linger in the air for a moment.

"Because... I wanted to." It's the most honest answer I can come up with at the moment. There are many reasons I shouldn't have, he's done more bad to me than good, but I said yes anyway. Why? Because even through all the bad, I feel like we belong together.

"That's a dumb answer."

"I guess I don't have anything smart to tell you. I just feel like we were meant to be. I can't explain why exactly. Maybe I'm just naive or stupid." I shrug. "Nic makes me feel alive and free, which is ironic, since he's basically locked me up since he kidnapped me. Hell, maybe I have Stockholm syndrome."

"Or maybe you got hit in the head one too many times," Lucas huffs.

"I'm not the one fighting on the weekend *for fun*."

"Is there a reason you came out here, or do you just get a thrill out of getting on my nerves?"

"I just wanted to thank you for coming, even if you didn't want to be here. It meant a lot to me you were here, and I hope that maybe in the future we can be... friends?"

"I don't have friends."

"Then maybe you need me more than you know."

"I don't need anyone, and I still don't like you," he snaps, flicking his cigarette several feet away.

"Do you still want to kill me?" At my words, Lucas tips his head back and looks into the sky like it holds all the answers. He doesn't say anything for so long, I think he is done talking to me.

Right before I'm about to walk away, he says, "I don't hate you anymore."

A smile tucks on my lips. It's a baby step, but it's a step, regardless. Lucas is still looking up into the sky, his arms hanging by his body. Taking the opportunity of him not seeing what I'm about to do, I drop my heels to the ground, throw my arms around him, and pull him in for a hug.

With my cheek pressed against his chest, I can hear his heart beating, which is the only sign that he is alive at all. His whole body is stiff, completely unmoving. I might as well be hugging a tree.

Surprisingly, he doesn't push me away. For a long moment, we remain in the most awkward hug of the century.

"You're so fucking annoying," Lucas finally breaks the silence, making me giggle.

I release him and step away, just in time to see the terrace door fly open.

Shit, I'm in trouble.

19

NIC

"For the tenth time, Nic, everything will be taken care of," Soo assures me. "Go to your little honeymoon and enjoy a moment of peace."

"Fine." I nod. "Where the hell is Celia. How long does it take her to take a damn dress off?"

One of the guards clears his throat to get my attention. "Sir, I think your wife went out onto the terrace."

"Motherfucker," I curse, pushing past Soo, who is already shaking his head.

I stomp through the house like I'm on a warpath—because I am. How could she lie to me? Today of all days.

I shove the terrace door open, and my eyes fall onto my brother and Celia, standing closer together than I appreciate. With my blood boiling, I cross the terrace and head for them. Celia takes a few more steps away from Lucas, her eyes pleading with me apologetically.

Too late for that princess.

"What the fuck?"

"I'm sorry. I just wanted to talk to him, that's all."

"You lied to me."

"I know. I was sure you wouldn't let me go if I hadn't." She isn't wrong, but that doesn't mean I'm any less furious.

I tear my eyes away from her and direct my glare at Lucas, who immediately shakes his head. "Don't even fucking look at me like that. We both know I didn't want to be here. I just came out here to enjoy a smoke."

"Nothing happened," Celia assures me while picking up her shoes from the grass. "We can go now. Let's just leave and start our honeymoon."

"Fine." I grab her hands and start pulling her away from Lucas. "But don't think I won't punish you for lying to me."

She doesn't say a word as I march her back inside and across the house to the front door. The car is already waiting for us. "Where are you taking me this time?" she asks as I settle her in the backseat.

Instead of answering her, I give her a punishing kiss and shut the door in her face. But sitting here, riding through town, isn't all I have planned for my little princess, not after what she did.

Once the car pulls away, I unbuckle my slacks and free my already hardened cock.

"What are you doing?" Her voice is breathy.

"Shut up and get your mouth on my cock," I order. When she doesn't move right away, I grab her by the back of her neck and force her head toward my dick. "Open."

She obeys, parting her lips for me to feed her my cock. I tilt up my hips and shove her head down, making her gag. Her manicured fingernails dig into my thigh, but she doesn't push me away. Instead, she moans around my cock.

"That's right, take me down your throat," I grunt, fucking her face in earnest. It doesn't take me long to come. Knowing she is my wife and now mine in every way has my balls tightening and jets of hot cum shooting into her throat.

"Fuck!" I pull out just a bit while I'm still coming, wanting her to taste my semen. "Don't swallow yet."

I pull her up to a sitting position. Her lipstick is smeared, and her mascara is running down her flushed cheeks in black streaks. She is the most beautiful creature I've ever seen.

"Show me."

Celia opens her mouth and shows me my cum on her tongue. "Now you can swallow." Again, she obeys me without question, and even though she doesn't quite deserve it, I want to reward her for sucking me off so well.

Tucking myself back into my slacks, I shift her hips sideways on the leather seats and slowly raise the hem of her white wedding gown.

I smirk as I work the dress up around her hips so I can remove her panties and open her thighs wider. When I settle my mouth over her heated flesh, she finally gets the picture.

Her hands cup my head as she leans against the car door for support. I don't give her lead up, going straight for her clit and sucking it between my teeth. She is so hot. In fact, she seems to burn hotter than the sun. The look in her eyes says she wants more, and when she whimpers, it feels like I've won something.

I angle her legs over my shoulders to make more room for me between her thighs without breaking contact with her cunt. She's dripping wet for me, and her legs are heated every time she involuntarily presses them to my cheeks. I delve my tongue into her opening and fuck her with it, leading her up to her orgasm with force. By the time she reaches the edge, she is shivering in my arms, and I'm fighting the urge to flip her over and plunge into her tight little channel. I was planning on taking my time with her tonight, making it all about her pleasure, but that ship sunk when she lied to me.

I plunge my tongue into her and add my hand to work on her clit with my thumb. She struggles and grinds into my face, her fingernails digging into my scalp, and I feel the first rhythmic pulse of her orgasm. She shatters with it, screaming and thrashing against me as I lick her hard to draw out the sensations.

When she's nothing but a pile of lace on the seat, arm draped over the edge of the leather, I finally lift my head. "Don't get too comfortable, *stellina*. I'm only getting started. You belong to me, forever, and I'm going to show you exactly what you have to look forward to."

20

CELIA

*W*hen the car stops, Nic exits to come around to my side and lifts me out.

"I can't walk, you know," I tell him, but truth be told, I'm not so sure. My entire body is still pulsing from the orgasm he gave me, and I'm not sure my knees know how to hold my weight up at the moment.

I stare up at the hotel we're walking into. It stretches far up into the sky until the ceiling of the hotel lobby cuts the sight off. Nic doesn't stop when we get inside, instead marching us straight to the bank of elevators on the far side of the lobby.

Inside, the soft lighting illuminates a beautiful space. If I had more time to sit and stare, I'd love to explore the art and the people. "This place is lovely. How did you find it?"

He nuzzles my ear and hits the elevator button. "It's my hotel. Well, I own a portion of it."

I rear away from him so I can see if he's serious. "You own a hotel?"

"Part of a hotel," he reminds me, carrying me into the elevator.

I shake my head. Who is this man? And where is the line in his life between the mainstream and the criminal? The thought that this lovely hotel might be a front for some kind of nefarious purpose makes me sad. Everything in my life turns out to be a facade.

"What's wrong, you were smiling, and then you weren't?" he says.

"Don't worry about it. I'm fine. I was just thinking."

The elevator dings loudly, and the doors slide open. He walks us inside, straight to a single door opposite the shiny chrome elevators. He balances me expertly as he scans the keycard and pushes the door open with his knee. Then he carries me into the hotel room and lets the door shut behind us.

The suite is even more beautiful than the lobby. The immediate room is a living room, complete with a bar and a big-screen TV. Off to the side is an enormous bathroom, a bedroom next to that, and opposite the door, one long bank of windows baring the city below in an incredible view.

"Wow," I breathe. "Look at that view."

I squirm in his arms to get him to put me down so I can explore. He carefully sets me on my feet before kneeling and carefully removing my shoes.

"Go, look. I'll order some food. I want you sated in every way tonight."

I can't help but think that declaration sounds naughty, and I like the possibilities. When he steps into the bedroom to call room service, I cross to the window. It's such a beautiful view. I can't wait to see it at full dark later. The sun has already sunk below the horizon, but there are still bright streaks of light in the sky right now.

The dress feels itchy across my shoulders. It's so beautiful, but the lace can chafe so easily.

Nic comes up behind me and boxes me in, his hands against the glass. "The food will be here soon. Do you want me to help you out of this dress?"

I nod. He goes to work on the zipper, and soon I'm standing in a pool of couture. My lingerie doesn't cover much, and of course, it's also white lace. A ridiculously impractical color, but I enjoy the way Nic is dragging his gaze up my body like he's never seen anything so beautiful.

"You're stunning," he whispers.

I slide my hands under the lapels of his tuxedo jacket and wrench it off his shoulders. His bow tie joins it. As he smiles, the corners of his eyes crinkle, and I can't help but smile back at him.

"Anything else you want me to help you slip out of?" he teases.

I shake my head. "Not until after we eat." My belly lets out a low rumble to punctuate my statement. We spend a few minutes just looking at each other, and for the first time, while I admire the hard lines of his body, I don't feel guilty.

Every other time he's touched me, and I enjoyed it, or when he kisses me, and I want more, it's always tempered with guilt and shame for wanting him, despite our too short and too rocky history.

But right now, I'm going to enjoy the way my husband is looking at me, and I'm going to enjoy touching him in return.

The doorbell rings, and he nudges me toward the couch while he goes to answer the door and collect the food.

When he returns, he carries a tray and sits it on the couch between us. They loaded the plates with various foods: steak, chicken, carbs of all shapes and sizes. A huge piece of cheesecake sits in the corner, and I eye it.

"Eat it if you want it."

I smile and grab the cake off the tray. He hands me a fork, which I use to devour half of it in a few big bites.

He's working on the steak when I dig into the chicken. It should feel ridiculous to sit here eating all this food in my underwear. And yet, I can't bring myself to care.

"Was it everything you wanted?" I ask him between bites. He'd made the wedding how he thought I wanted it, but was it what he wanted too?

The fork pauses on the way to his mouth. "The only thing I wanted at the wedding was you. I'm happy."

I consider his answer while I finish eating. Part of me thinks I shouldn't be so pleased by the way he said, 'I'm happy.'

After he finishes his food, he takes the tray to a table by the door and washes his hands in the bathroom sink.

I head into the bedroom and inspect this new space. The view in this room is equally lovely, so I climb up on the bed and lie down so I can stare out at the skyline. It makes up the entire view past the end of the bed.

Nic enters a moment later, now only in his boxer briefs, and walks around the bed to climb in beside me. He lies down next to me and gathers me into the curve of his shoulder.

When I place my hand on his chest, I feel the heavy thump of his heart under my palm. Feeling bold and deciding that for once, I'm not going to wait for him to turn me inside out, I run my hand down his chest to his belly.

"What are you doing, *stellina*?" he asks, his tone full of humor.

I shrug. "Exploring my husband, I suppose."

He doesn't say anything more when I tuck my hand under the waistband of his boxer briefs. His cock is already hard, and I reach in and draw him out. To make it easier, he wiggles out of his underwear to toss them away.

Now, I can really look at him. He's thick and long and growing harder as I explore him with my fingers.

I sit up and shuffle down so I can take him in my mouth. When I look up the line of his body, he locks eyes with me. I'm not sure what I see in his gaze, but it's different from the way he usually looks at me. There's something softer there, something warmer.

I gently lick his head and slide my mouth around it and give him a lingering suck.

He arches his hips toward me. And in that moment, for the first time, I feel a sense of power, of control, I've never felt before.

I want more. More of the salty taste of him. More of his ragged breathing. More of his fingers tangled in my hair. Bobby pins slip out of my tresses and pool around us on the white bedspread.

I lower my head and take more of him. When I gag, he tugs me back up. But I don't give up that easily. I try again, this time taking him deeper.

"Relax your throat, princess, and you can take all you want. Remember when you did before?"

I grip the base of him and shift to anchor over the top of him. Then I slide my mouth down his length again until, finally, I can brush my nose against his hip. His ragged pant turns into a grunt as I rise up and repeat the motion.

Each sound he makes amps me further. I'm so wet, just fucking him with my mouth. I feel so fucking powerful and sexy taking him like this.

Both of his hands spear my hair now, and I increase my pace. Using both hands and my mouth to work him faster and faster.

"I'm going to come, *stellina*. Would you like that? Want me to pour my cum down that pretty throat?"

I can only moan in answer as he gently helps me maintain my tempo. It only takes a few more minutes, and then he comes with a heavy growl, his hands fisting my hair, and his cum pulsing down my throat.

When he slumps flat on the bedding again, I pull off his still erect cock and lick the last beads of his cum from the tip. But it's not enough for me. I want more of him, all of him, and I'm so ready to take it.

I peel off my panties and bra and toss them to the floor. He watches me with an amused look on his face. Then I crawl up to his thighs, throw one leg over, and run myself along the hard length of him. Not inside yet, not all the way. The moment I do, I know he won't be content to let me stay in control.

"I like a woman with a plan," he says, cupping my hips to steady me.

I fumble with trying to hold on to him and sink down his length, so he helps. He grips himself in one hand and helps me lower onto his length with the other. The stretch burns bright for a flash of a second, and then pleasure chases it away, spreading along my nerves until I'm fully seated on him.

His smile is warm as he watches me. "What now?"

I tentatively lift my hips so I can figure out the mechanics of this position. Each angle and way I shift my upper body causes a different sensation. I find the one that makes him choke out a moan and stick with that one.

I fist my hands on his upper belly as I use him to lift my hips up and down at a steadier pace.

His fingers dig into my hips as I chase my orgasm, looming on the horizon. Just as I'm about to tumble over the edge, he drags me onto him and holds me tight so I can't move.

"What the hell?"

He laughs, then rolls me over in one smooth motion, so he's on top of me, his cock still buried deep inside me. Not even missing a beat, he picks up the pace I had, but this time harder and faster. Each slam of his hips into mine sends me sliding up the bed toward the pillow mountain in front of the headboard.

"Your turn, *stellina*," he whispers, staring down at my face.

We lock gazes as he pounds into me, and I arch my hips up to meet him. And then I shatter. Everything in me breaks open, bright and shining. Wave after wave of pleasure pours through my body, and all I can do is hold on to him and ride it out. When I come back to myself, he's lying with his weight partially on me, his head on my chest, and his heavy breathing tickles the sweaty skin across my belly.

When I can finally form words again, I mumble, "I need water."

He rises as if his entire world wasn't just shifted on its axis and brings me a bottle of water. Once I sit up and down most of the bottle, he lifts me and carries me into the bathroom.

When I catch sight of where he's about to place me, I let out a giddy laugh. A jacuzzi tub sits in the middle of the floor, and he lowers me into the bowl and turns toward the faucets. The water warms quickly, and he settles into the bathtub behind me as it fills.

There is a selection of bubble baths along the edge of the tub, and I open them all, choosing several to dump into the tub.

"You know when I turn on the jets, the bubbles are going to grow exponentially," he says.

I nod. "Let's do it."

He hits the button, and the jets start with a rumble. Almost immediately, the bubbles multiply, creating a huge foam cap on top of the water. I slap at the bubbles, batting them down so they don't overwhelm us.

I know my face must be goofy with the smile there. Bubble baths are one of my favorite things.

"I'll get you bubbles for our house," he tells me, whispering in my ear.

I shift so I can meet his eyes. "I would love that."

"I can tell. You look happy right now."

As if he admitted something he didn't want to, his face clears to a neutral look. "I'll make sure they stay on the shopping list for you. As I told you, it's my pleasure to take care of all of your needs."

He drops his mouth to my ear and slides his lips down to my neck.

"All my needs, huh?"

When he bites the side of my neck, I press back into him.

"All of them, princess. I can't wait to learn them all so I can ensure I'm doing a good job."

His fingers dip down my belly, into the folds of my pussy. I shudder and arch my hips forward, loving the way he teases me. I'm still sensitive from my last orgasm, but I don't want to wait for more.

I turn in the water so I can wrap my arms around his neck. He brings his hands up to my waist to support me as the water threatens to float me to the other end of the tub.

"What about your needs?" I ask.

He smiles. A true smile, and it's enough to melt things inside my chest. "What needs do you mean?"

I drop a hand and grip him. "Well, I've figured out one of them. How about you let me know if there are more I can assist with?"

His eyes grow dark, and his grin naughty. "Right now, I need to finish this bath so I can fuck you again. Let me wash you, and then we'll see about the rest."

21

NIC

Celia is settling into my house like she owns it. Sarah still gives her lip, and I can tell Celia likes it when she pushes back. It's been a couple of weeks since the wedding, and the first few days, I worried she'd change her mind, walk out in the middle of the night, or demand to leave.

But she doesn't. She buys new clothes, all approved by me, of course, and reorganizes our closet. When she picked out a new rug for the bedroom, she looked almost worried I'd revoke the credit card I gave her. But I've never been good with that sort of shit, and I told her she can redecorate the entire house if she wants to.

Now the doubt has eased. I should focus on Ricci and how to finally bring him down. Literally, kill the last barrier between Celia giving me her heart and both of us exacting our revenge. When I told her she can kill Ricci when the time comes, I wasn't exactly honest. I have no intention of letting her be like me, her soul tainted, blood on her hands. She might hate me for a little while after it's done, but it'll be worth it to keep her innocent and safe.

Soo is waiting in my office when I enter in the morning. He's sitting in the usual chair opposite my desk. But today, he looks a little more disheveled than usual. His usually tidy hair is brushed away from his face like he's been running his hands through it repeatedly. Something is eating at him.

"You're up early."

He tosses a stack of paper on my desk, and I swing around, take my chair, and look at what he's brought me.

"I never went to sleep last night. As you can see, I've gotten some disturbing news."

Each sheet in the hefty stack is an individual email. Some of them from Ricci, some of them from one of the Gardello boys. Even a couple from the reclusive Bianci, who rarely leaves his lakeside mansion.

"Let's pretend I'm going to read every single one of these. Can you give me the quick version? I'm assuming it explains why you look like shit."

Soo leans his head back in the chair and closes his eyes. "Basically, they say the five families have been meeting in secret for a while via secure video chat, and right now, they have two targets: you and your new bride."

I sit forward and spread the emails out on the surface of my desk. "Did they threaten her?" Threats to me are nothing. I'm used to it. But if they so much as breathe her name in the same sentence as a threat, I'm suddenly going to get a lot more motivated to rip their heads off one by one.

"No, but I assume any threat to you is a threat to her, too. I suggest we keep her indoors and secure, so we don't give them a chance."

Even though my heart is still pounding in my chest, I relax again. "Does your spy know anything about when these meetings occur?"

Soo shakes his head. "Nope, she would have told me. She's very thorough."

I don't touch that comment. Especially since I witnessed him in her presence a while ago, and I know something is going on there. He hasn't been ready to say anything yet, and I won't push.

"Do you think Celia knows anything about these online meetings?"

This gets his attention. He pops one eye open and looks at me. "Maybe? You should ask her. I know she was unwilling to give us intel when she first arrived here, but her circumstances have changed, and she might know more than she thinks."

I shove out of the chair and head toward the door. "Get some sleep. I'll talk to her."

"No, I'll come too, so you don't have to repeat things later."

When I last saw her, she told me she planned to spend the morning in the library. Soo follows me down, and we find her lying on the couch with a book tucked against her knees.

She looks up when I enter, a smile on her lips that shoots straight into my chest. When Soo comes up behind me, she closes the book in her lap, keeping her finger between the pages to mark her place. "What's going on?"

I sit beside her, and Soo stands nearby to watch us. "I wanted to ask if you know anything about the virtual meetings the five families have been having?"

She shakes her head and leans up to resettle her legs underneath her. "No, it's news to me. My father hates using his laptop and used to get angry he couldn't read his emails."

Soo asks the next question. "Do you know anything that might help us get to him? Anything you might not have told us before, maybe out of spite, or to protect him?"

She narrows her eyes at him. "No, I would have said something. I was trained to be a trophy wife. They didn't tell me anything. Why would they? Most of what I know about the five families revolves around dinner parties and wine choices. All pretty silly and mundane things. My mom used to quiz me on family tastes, food allergies, gossip that might affect seating charts."

Soo drags the coffee table closer to the couch and perches on the edge, so he can focus his attention on her.

She watches him with wide eyes and glances back at me. I give her an encouraging nod. "Tell him what you know, don't worry about it."

When she focuses on Soo again, he leans forward to force her eye contact. "Tell me."

She shakes her head. "You're going to have to ask a question or be specific. My head is full of useless stuff, and I can't just spew it all out to you."

Soo nods. "Let's start with the gossip, then. Most of that sort of thing is worthless, but it might give us something useful, and I can vet the info easy enough."

"Well, they say the Gardello family is broke. That the sons have plowed through their trust funds and their family money trying to outfit their casinos and on hookers. It's why I was supposed to marry into the family, they wanted to get their hands on my father's money, and he was paying them a sort of dowry."

I nod. "We knew that one already. But yes, stuff like that, what else do you have?"

She smiles and leans in conspiratorially. "There is talk that the Greco siblings, they are twins, are closer than they should be as twins. And they also say they are the reason the father is on home care and can no longer make his own decisions."

Soo meets my eyes and shakes his head. Yeah, I hadn't known this little tidbit either. "We knew the twins are running the family and that the father is an invalid, but we didn't know that they might be the reason he's dying. Or about the other side of things."

"Weird, right? I don't know if they are sleeping together, but the rumors say they might be."

"What else?" Soo prompts.

She shrugs. "Well, my mom says the Marino family is one breath away from destruction. The father dotes on the daughter and ignores the sons. They resent him, even though they love their sister, and they might want to overthrow their father to take over the family. It was all threaded with 'make sure you don't sit the sons by the father,' but yeah, it's all very soap opera at their house, apparently."

"That's good," Soo says, nodding.

She continues. "Bianci is the only one I haven't met before. He's reclusive, and he's never been to any of the dinners. While they never all come to the house at once, I've at least met all the families individually, except him. When I was a kid, I met his father, but not the son, not after his father died. So, of course, everyone is curious about him and how he's changed his territory since his father's death."

As she speaks, my heart squeezes tighter in my chest. I bounce my gaze between her and Soo, noticing how eager she is to help us. It's a far cry from when I first brought her here, and she refused to give me any information about her father. But as we sit here, and she keeps talking to Soo, I realize she hasn't given us any information about him yet. Just about the other members of the five families.

When she stops speaking, and Soo yawns, his eyes growing heavy, I wave at them. They both look my way, and I give Soo a nod. He stands and heads for the door without another word.

"Go get some sleep and come find me when you wake up," I call after him.

He closes the door behind him, and I turn all my attention to Celia. She stares at me expectantly, as if waiting for my own questions, and I have them.

I reach out and grasp her by the waist to drag her into my lap. She resettles on top of my legs and leans her head against my chest. It's a position we take often, as I know how much she likes to be held. And to be honest, I enjoy holding her like this; it comforts me. Cementing the fact that she belongs to me in every way.

After a moment, she lifts her face so she can look at me. "Are you angry with me?"

I shake my head. "No, I'm not upset with you. I'm just trying to figure out why you didn't tell us any of this information sooner. Right now, I can't say if it will be useful. But I also can't say if it would have been useful sooner. Things have changed since you were originally taken. Things that were true then might no longer be true."

"In my defense, I was held captive. Why would I help my kidnappers in any way?"

I run my hand down her back and resettle her against my chest. Something I also noticed, she shares more when she doesn't have to meet my eyes when she does it. "I can understand that logic. I know you won't do anything to deliberately hurt me. I also know you want your own revenge against your father. But you didn't give Soo any information about him."

Her breath fans across my neck, and I wait for her to answer.

"You were going to sell me. As far as I was concerned, you were just as much an enemy as anyone else."

It's further reasoning for why she didn't share the other information with us, but again, nothing about her father. "Celia?"

She huffs. "It's because of Lucas."

"Watch the attitude, princess. What does my brother have to do with you sharing information about your father?"

When she doesn't answer, I grip her hips and deposit her back on the couch so I can look into her eyes. She might share less, but she also knows when not to push me. And I need her to see I'm serious about getting an answer. "Celia, answer me. What does this information about your father have to do with Lucas?"

She tries to look away, but I capture her chin and drag her gaze back to mine.

"It's because when he gets any sort of information that he can act on, he's going to make a move on him."

It's hard for me to fault her logic. I've known Lucas wants to go after Ricci for a while. It was his entire plan by taking Celia before. However, I was not aware Celia had become so attuned to Lucas and his motivations. It makes me want to kill him all over again.

"You are right. If Lucas gets any kind of information he can use, he'll go straight for your father. Which is why I've had Soo watching him since the moment you requested we release him. All his activities are under constant surveillance."

She shakes her head. "Didn't you have him under surveillance before, and he was able to kidnap me right from under your noses at your own auction?"

When she puts it like that, it makes my team seem incompetent. Something I neither like nor appreciate. My fingers tighten on her chin. "Well, what do you propose we do about him, then? And if you have any information that might help us get to your father, Soo, nor I, are dumb enough to share it with Lucas. Especially knowing how close to the edge of doing something irrational he is."

We sit in silence for a moment, and I hate the look of worry in her eyes. I know it's more about losing another family member than Lucas himself. She hasn't had enough time with him to develop that sort of relationship. But I know she wants to, if Lucas will let her in. I also don't have the heart to tell her it's unlikely. Neither of us are the tender-loving types.

"I had a thought, but I know if I ask you to do it, he'll hate me forever." She's wringing her hands as if she's been worried about whatever it is for some time.

"Tell me, princess."

A tear slips down her cheek. "I know the irony of me asking this, trust me, but will you and Soo lock him up again? It's the only thing I can think of that might make sure he stays safe while we get into position to take my father down."

I nod and drag her back into my arms. "You're right. If he knew you asked me that, he would hate you. Even more so, if I do it, and he finds out you requested it."

"I can live with the consequences if it means he's alive at the end of all this," she whispers.

My brave princess. I clutch her tighter. "We are all going to be alive at the end of this, don't worry."

I still haven't had the heart to tell her that if she is the one who takes her father's life, Lucas will also hate her. Either way it happens, she's not going to get the relationship with him she craves.

22

CELIA

I honestly can't believe I asked Nic to lock up his own brother. Maybe part of me believed he wouldn't do it, and he hasn't, but he says it's because Lucas will hate me if he finds out. But also because he wants to repair his own relationship with him.

I get it, but it doesn't make it any easier to hear. Whenever Lucas comes to the house to deliver something to Soo or briefly fight with Nic, he ignores me completely as if I don't exist. I can't figure out why he's so adamant about not speaking with me. Obviously, it's likely because of my parentage, but to be fair, it's his parentage too, and I don't hold that against him.

I'm standing in the closet surveying my clothing. Nic told me I didn't need to dress for dinner, which means we likely aren't going out. Come to think of it, he hasn't let me out of the house, even on the lawn, since our honeymoon. Not that I've asked to go anywhere, but it seems curious. My safety is his top priority. He's made that very clear since I arrived. But I also can't let him keep me locked up, or he might never let me out.

Things have changed so much between us, so much so that he seems proud of me. Proud that I'm helping in his plans, that I'm part of his world, or at the very least, no longer running from him. I crave the looks he gives me when he thinks I'm not looking: part sheer need and part awe. But the ones filled with hope and pride are the best.

I'm tangled up inside about this even while I want his hands on me every minute and his soft whispers in my ear. Even now, I'm staring at my clothes fucking mooning over the man. I need to get my shit together; it's not always going to be like this. Once he has whatever he wants from me, once he's satisfied his lust or his curiosity, he'll put me up in a penthouse somewhere and forget I exist. I know how this world operates. No one has a happy marriage, and I refuse to be some sort of prize for his misdeeds.

I leave my clothes alone and decide to wear the leggings and sweater combo I already have on. Nic won't care, as long as he can strip it off me when we're done eating. Sometimes, he can't wait and will even start during dinner. If it's been a long day, and he hasn't been able to touch me in a while—like waiting is too much for him to bear.

My heart flutters at the thought of him bending me over the polished wood of the dining room table. Again. He ignites things in me I didn't even know were there. Whenever his hands touch my skin, I can't think about anything else. Maybe that's how he likes it, and he's trying to keep my head muddled by lust, so I don't notice what's going on around the house.

I sit on the bed and wait for Nic to come find me. He's been late the last couple of nights. He and Soo have been planning some mysterious activities. When I asked about it, all he said was it had to do with the five families and not specifically my father, so I don't need to worry about it.

He obviously doesn't know me well enough yet if he thinks I won't worry just because he ordered me not to.

Nic enters the bedroom a few moments later, and it takes everything in me not to reach out for him and have him wrap me in his arms.

"Are you ready to eat? I think Sarah said the food is done and on the table. We won't be disturbed."

I nod and take his offered arm. He leads me to the dining room, sits me in the chair next to his before taking his own seat. There are only two plates covered with trays, silverware, water, and wine sitting out. Good. I'm not in the mood to deal with anyone else at dinner tonight.

"Are you all right?" he asks, lifting the tray off his food and setting it aside.

"Yes, I'm just thinking about whatever it is you and Soo are working on. I just worry, and yes, I know you told me not to, but I'm going to do it, anyway. Will you share your plan with me, or are you guys keeping it all to yourselves?"

I've forced cheer in my tone, and I know he hears it. It can't be helped. I lift the tray off my food and tip it over, so the condensation doesn't escape all over the table, and set it beside my plate. As usual, Sarah's team made a delicious dinner. Chicken, vegetables, and a small salad.

I grab my fork and eye the food, hoping Nic will answer my question so I don't have to ask him again or try a damn lifeline to get it.

I spear some of the chicken and nibble on it. He's eating with relish, he always does, beside me, and I shake my head as I swallow my food.

No, he's not going to answer, and I'm going to have to try a different tactic to get it. I place my fork on the table and stare at him until he lifts his gaze to mine.

"Please, don't do this to me. Don't shut me out."

He drops his fork to his plate. "Princess," he warns.

"Do you have a plan together?"

Grinding his jaw, he finally answers me. "Yes, Soo and I came up with a plan. We decided that in order to bring your father down, we need to destabilize his base of power first. We need to use the other families to bring him down, and then we can conduct a more focused strike against him. So right now, we are reviewing the families for weaknesses to see who we can hit first and with minimal setup."

I go back to eating, my chest lighter now that he's talking to me. "Do you already have one in mind? Do you want my suggestion?"

Now that I'm back to shoveling food in my mouth, he resumes eating his own meal. After he swallows, he nods. "We decided we don't need to hit all five—we just need the majority of three to ensure we have what we need to take him down. Once we get three families to side with us, we'll be able to finish him off."

I pause in bringing my fork to my mouth. "Side with you? You're going to try to negotiate with these people? I'm not sure if you know this, but they are all liars and criminals. They will say one thing and do another."

His tone is icy when he says, "Princess, I'm a liar and a criminal. I've dealt with my kind before, and I know how to ensure they won't double-cross us once the plan is in motion."

It's a warning and a reminder in case I ever forget what kind of man he is. I straighten my shoulders, put my fork on the table, and shove my chair back. "I'm not hungry anymore. I think I'll go up to bed."

I only make it to the door before he stops me by grabbing me around the hips and carrying me back to the table, settling me on his lap. "Tell me what's wrong," he orders.

Tears are building, and I'm not even sure why. "You're keeping the details from me, and then you say that you're a criminal and a liar like you need to remind me constantly that you aren't a perfect man. You don't think I know that?"

He tugs me into his embrace, and while I resist, he wins. He always wins. I let my arms hang by my side as he hugs me tight to his chest. "I wasn't trying to deliberately keep anything from you. We are targeting the Marino family first. Based on the information you gave us and Soo's spy network, we've discovered they are the most unstable."

I nod against his chest, happy at least the tears didn't win and embarrass me further. "When is it all happening?"

"Tonight," he says.

I jerk from his grasp to look up at him. "Tonight? What? When?"

"We set a meeting with both the Marino boys and the DEA agent who helps their father run guns through trade shows. If we can come to an arrangement, we can set it up so that they walk away with their family's power, and we walk away with an alliance."

I'm still not understanding how they could have put this entire plan into motion already. We were just talking about him and Soo checking on my information this morning. Why the urgency? I don't have the courage to ask or pry further, though.

"Eat. You look a little pale, and I know you didn't eat much at lunch today. Don't make me force you."

I glare at him. "How do you know what I did or didn't eat at lunch? If Sarah is reporting on my eating habits, she and I are about to have an uncomfortable conversation for both of us."

"No, but watch your tone before I decide you need another lesson in respect. We may be married now, but that doesn't mean you can let that bratty mouth run free."

He deposits me in front of my plate again. "I've just been stressed out about you plotting and planning, and me not knowing what the hell is happening. I don't enjoy being out of the loop about things. It makes me feel like a prisoner all over again, especially since you haven't taken me anywhere in a while or let me out of the house."

"I'm only trying to keep you safe. You don't need to know every detail."

I take a huge bite of my roll and chew, so I have time to think of a tactful response to that. Will I be safe after he brings down the five families? Or after my father is dead? Or maybe at some other random point in the future that he hasn't disclosed for me? I don't doubt he cares for me in his own way, but I also fear being locked up in his house until I die because he doesn't want anything to happen to me.

"I appreciate you wanting me to be safe, but I'm not fragile, and I'm not going to break. I also doubt there are snipers on the lawn or anything, so maybe let up so I can at least go outside the house?"

He chews his own food and stares me down. "No. Not until the threat has passed."

His tone is hard and leaves no room for argument. After that, we finish our meal relatively quickly and in silence. We've only been married for around a month, and I already feel like our meals are those of an old married couple who have been together all of their lives.

He tries to hold my hand as he escorts me back to our bedroom, but I rush ahead of him, knowing he'll make me pay for it later. Once inside, I sit on the edge of the bed and watch as he prepares for his meeting. He changes his suit and cleans up his hair. He's too fucking beautiful.

Worry claws at my chest again. "Soo is going to be there with you, right? Will you have more back up? Do you have a plan for when things go south?"

He chuckles as he adjusts his tie until I throw up my hands and stalk toward him to help him myself. Once it's perfect, I smooth my hands down his lapels and use them to drag his face more level with mine. I kiss him and pull away. "If you ever want to touch me again, you'll stay safe and come back in one piece."

The edge of his mouth turns up into a wicked grin. "Are you worried about me, a common criminal, princess?"

I glare and shove him away again, going back to sit on the bed. That's when I notice a little black box on the covers I didn't see before.

"Open it," he says, "it's a gift."

Inside is a sleek black hand radio. I turn it over in my palms, inspecting it. "What's it for?"

"It's because I know you will be worried from the second I walk out the door. This way, you'll be able to listen to the team's communications about what is happening."

The gesture loosens something near my heart. Fuck. When did he get so thoughtful? And why does it make me want to strip his clothes off?

A moment later, Soo knocks on the door, and both men leave.

I curl up on the bed with the walkie-talkie next to me on top of the pillow. The plan seems relatively simple by what I hear as the night progresses. They set one meeting with the dirty DEA agent and bribed him so that he will only work with the Marino sons. After that, they set another meeting with the Marino boys to make sure they are on board with the plan.

As I listen to the security team rumble back-and-forth, it truly hits me just how well organized Nic's teams really are. It gives me some sense of relief about how his plans might go. Especially the ones that will eventually involve my father.

I listen to the radio until the teams say they are heading home. And then I take it with me when I go down to the foyer and wait for them to walk in. Soo enters first, and I ignore him. When Nic clears the threshold, I launch myself at him and wrap my arms around his neck. He lifts me up in his arms so I can hug him tighter and wrap my legs around his lower back.

He doesn't say anything to Soo, only walks me up the stairs to our bedroom, where he gently eases me down to the bed. "It's late. You shouldn't have waited up."

I swipe at his chest. "You know damn well I wouldn't have been able to go to sleep until I knew you returned home safely."

He leans in and nibbles my bottom lip. "Well, princess, I'm home safely. Now let me show you what I've been thinking about since the moment I walked out the door tonight."

Then he sinks to his knees on the floor and spreads my thighs.

23

NIC

I know she feels confined in the house, but I can't allow her to leave. If anything happens to her, I don't know what I will do with myself or the blinding rage that would follow in the wake of her loss.

Now that the plan is in motion, I feel even more possessive of her. If any of the families get word we are making a move. If Ricci gets word... it might mean they take the offensive. That would put her even more in danger. Soo is careful with his information. It's the security teams I always worry about. They have been fully vetted, paid well, and are loyal to Soo and me, but Soo is the only person I trust. Unfortunately, he can't take on everything alone like the old days when we were first building our empire.

I know Celia is worried for me, and yet, all I can think about is her safety. If she truly knew how close I am to putting her on a jet and locking her in a big house on the other side of the world, she would be furious with me. The thought only crosses my mind about a hundred times a day.

Celia walks into my office in another little sundress, and I watch as she treks from the door to my chair. If she sees the hunger in my eyes, she doesn't comment on it.

"You wanted me to come talk to you after breakfast?"

I settle her on my lap and shift her so I can look into her eyes when I speak. When she leaves my office today, I need to be very sure she understands everything I'm about to explain to her. "As you are very aware, we've started our plan to take down your father. Now, I also need to ensure you always remain safe. That no matter what happens, no one can get to you."

I hate the fear in her eyes as I talk. Even more so, knowing that once I finish, she has the means to leave me forever. I've gone out of my way to make sure she understands that she can't escape me. And now, I'm just going to hand her the knowledge and ability to do so.

I just have to hope that she'll keep her word and stay with me.

She shifts on my lap. "Whatever it is, just say it. You're scaring me."

"Some time ago, I put in motion a plan to ensure your safety if somehow your father succeeds in killing me."

Her hands rush up to grip my cheeks. "Don't say things like that."

"As much as I like to think about our success. I also have to think about our failure, and the ultimate failure would be to let the five families take you after I'm gone."

Again, she shakes her head frantically. "I don't like this. What are you saying?"

"Only that there are a few things you need to be made aware of. The first of which is the tunnel system under the house. It leads out about a half-mile to the edge of the property. If something happens, and the house is taken, you can escape via that route. There is a vehicle parked at the mouth of the tunnel that will have everything you need for your escape."

She stares at me wide-eyed.

"I need you to nod or acknowledge that you understand what I'm saying."

When she doesn't, I lift her by the hips up onto the edge of the desk and shove my chair back. At this angle, I can look into her eyes better. And she can see how serious I am.

"I hope you will never have to touch this option. But I need you to understand that they are in place for your safety. Now be a good girl and tell me you understand."

After a heartbeat, she nods. "I understand. I don't like it, but I understand."

"You don't have to like it."

I gently pick her up and lower her to the floor again. Then I lead her out of my office, through the house, and down the basement steps. We pass the laundry room, and she stares around until we stop at a heavy wooden door on the other side of the basement.

"This is the door you will use to make your escape if you need it. It stays locked, but the keys are in the safe in my office. Along with the keys, you'll find a passport and money, anything you might need to make a clean getaway."

This time I don't have to prompt her response. She nods, and I hug her tight to my chest.

"I've written down the access code to the safe and a phone number to someone I know outside the city who can help you if you need it."

I hate everything about this. The thought of losing her is like taking a knife to the gut. But I don't know how to tell her what she means to me without scaring her.

We walk back up to the main house and into my office. Once inside, I guide her to the hatch in the floor behind my desk and explain how to open the safe. I have no doubt she will be able to figure it out on her own, but instructing her makes me happy, so I carry on.

Once I'm finished, I turn to her, knowing that she is going to be angry with me in a few seconds. "In a few hours, I'm going to be leaving to meet with Bianci."

"What?" Her gaze widens. "I should be there with you."

My insides twist. "I can't have you there. The risk of word getting back to your father is too high."

"Word about what?"

"What do you think your father will do if he gets his hands on you after you married the man targeting him? He killed your sister for less." I feel like a dick for reminding her of what she lost, but she needs to take this seriously.

She considers my question for a moment, and her pretty brown eyes fill with confusion a second before she answers. "I think he would try to use me against you." Her voice deflates completely as understanding of what may happen sinks in. A deep frown mars her face. "I just hate the thought of you out there alone."

Her admission makes my chest tighten, and I lean into her, kissing the edge of her mouth, trying to soothe some of the fear away. "I won't be alone. Soo will be with me, and we have his very well-trained security team along for the ride. Everything will be fine."

If her arguments weren't a demonstration of how much she cares, I would punish her for it. But how can I, when her fears reflect my own?

"I want to believe you, but..."

I shake my head and grasp her chin with two fingers, wanting her to see and hear my words fully. "Shhh, let's spend the rest of the evening in bed together."

A lustful haze swallows up the fear previously reflecting in the pools of her brown eyes. And there's no place I would rather be. I can only hope that everything goes as planned.

WHEN MY ALARM goes off a few hours later, I give Celia a quick kiss, casting her naked body in a sweeping glance. My cock is already hardening again, remembering all the things I did to her body a few hours ago. I barely shake the lustful haze and draw to climb back into bed away and get dressed before heading downstairs to meet Soo.

"I'd say good morning, but I'm not sure you even slept," Soo says on a yawn, like, he too, didn't sleep—for a completely different reason.

If he was anyone else, I might slug him in the face, but there is no one like Soo. My best friend and confidant.

I smirk. "I slept perfectly fine, thank you for asking."

We climb into the blacked-out SUV and head across town toward the industrial park. It's only a short ride to the meeting location Bianci requested. We arrive a few minutes early and sit in the SUV, waiting for the mysterious Bianci to make his appearance known.

The man who shows up just seconds from being late is not at all what I expect. We exit our SUV at the same time he exits his. The man is tall and lanky with black hair, and his clothes are more suited to a college gamer than an international criminal.

He approaches Soo and me alone. We chose to meet at an abandoned parking lot at the edge of town, and I wonder for his sanity that he would come out here by himself.

"So, you are the ones giving everyone trouble? I'm excited to meet you," he says, holding his hand out for us to shake.

Soo and I share a look between us, then shake the man's hand. Because we are both at a loss for words, I let Soo take the lead on this one.

"We want you to join us in our plan to remove Ricci as head of the five families."

Bianci cocks his head to the side as he studies us. "Why should I do that? And please, don't mistake it as a threat. I'm genuinely curious about what you will say."

It's my turn. "Because Ricci has lost his touch. Also, I just really want to kill him. Without going into a family saga, just know it's warranted."

A smile plays on Bianci's mouth. "Well, it just so happens that I don't support Ricci in his power, and I've been hunting my own way to remove him from the city's criminal throne. It looks like you boys have already gotten started, though. I'm an only child, and when my father's territory fell to me, Ricci hasn't exactly approved of how I shifted my father's business to the digital age. In fact, I think it's time all the old guard takes a back seat and lets their children reform the five families into a modern era."

Soo speaks up. "We need some kind of assurance that you're serious about your commitment. Otherwise, you could just be talking out of your ass and playing us while you run back to Ricci to report."

He nods and shucks a backpack off his shoulders I hadn't even noticed. The security team goes for their guns, but Soo waves them off as the man digs a laptop from his bag.

"While conducting my own search into Ricci's affairs, I found an interesting little corner of the world." He types while holding the bottom of his laptop one-handed.

Then he spins the computer to face us and highlights a portion of text on what looks like a darknet chat room.

"I'm not sure if you are aware, but there weren't always five families. At one point, we were six. And that sixth family ruled the other five. Until they were murdered several years ago. I was away at school most of my life, so I didn't get a crash course in this world until my father passed. However, I think that this little tidbit of information about the murder of this family might be enough to ignite the other leaders into helping your cause."

I share another look with Soo and close the laptop, handing it back toward Bianci. While disclosing information about my identity might earn me a measure of trust from this man, it would also mean going back on a promise I made to myself a long time ago. I'm a Diavolo. When I took the name and built my empire, I vowed to never look back. At least not until my family's lives are avenged. What right do I have to that name with their killer still roaming free?

He waves me off. "No, you keep it. The information about that chat server is on there, maybe you can find something interesting there that I missed, or at the very least, it might give you some more context."

When he slips his backpack on again, he gives us an expectant look. "Are we done here?"

"Yes, thank you." I shake his hand, and so does Soo. Then he walks away like he doesn't have a care in the world.

I wait until we're both back in the car before I bring him up. "Did he seem all there to you?"

Soo starts the car, and we pull away, heading back toward the house. "He seems interesting. Also, I think he knows more than he shared with us. If he has access to all of the five family networks, he might know a lot of secrets. Which makes him an excellent ally."

As usual, Soo isn't wrong.

The city passes around me in a blur, but my mind is back in that house the day I watched the light leave my mother's eyes.

"Are you ever going to tell Celia about who you really are?" Soo asks.

I turn to look at my friend. "She knows who I am. I'm a Diavolo, and now so is she."

He doesn't bring it up again, and I'm grateful. Dwelling on the past doesn't ensure the future.

When we return to the house, he heads off with the laptop, leaving me to go find Celia. I smile, thinking about stripping her of whatever lacy thing she's wearing as I bound up the stairs. She's sitting on our bed again when I enter.

She looks up as I close the door. "How did it go?"

I strip off my jacket and my shirt, tossing them in the closet. "It went better than I expected."

"But?" she prompts.

I shake my head and climb up beside her on the bed so I can draw her into my arms. "But nothing. He was already on board with our plan when we arrived. It seems he's been trying to find a way to restructure the five families for some time."

I don't tell her about what he said regarding the sixth family. It's not important yet. I'm not that boy anymore.

"You seem like you want to say more but aren't sure how."

I shake my head, even though she can't see it, and kiss the top of hers. "No, I'm fine, I'm just thinking. He gave us some good information, and now we need to figure out how to use it to our advantage. That's half the job."

"Are you sur—"

"Celia, drop it." My tone is clipped, but I don't regret it.

She stiffens in my arms and pulls away. Her distance only makes me angrier. I push off the bed and head out of the room toward my office. At the very least, I can get some work done while I consider Bianci.

When I settle in my chair and dig my phone out of my pocket, I find a text message from an unknown number. On the screen is an image of an email sent from what has to be a dummy account. The body of the email makes me stop breathing for a moment.

The text is from Bianci, and it says that Ricci knows the plan is in motion and is already fortifying for future events.

It wasn't as if I thought we'd get to the endgame of this thing unscathed. Nor did I expect Ricci to stay ignorant of my plan. However, I wish I had more time. At the very least, more time to help Celia come to terms with what is about to happen. She may say she wants to pull that trigger, but there's nothing that can prepare you for taking a life for the first time. I don't want that stain on her soul, and I know the moment I take it from her, she's going to hate me.

She'll get over it, eventually. But I know the soft kisses and midnight whispers will disappear at the same time. And if she ever trusts me again, I'll still have ruined the best thing in my life.

Is it worth it to lose her just to take down Ricci? Some time ago, my revenge was the only thing driving me, the only thing getting me out of bed in the morning. And now, it's Celia's smile that drags me up from the nightmares. It's touching her cheek and smelling her hair after she washes it.

All the gentle, non-sexual intimacy we've built over the last month or so will be tainted by her father's death. Marred by it, and I don't know if I can allow it.

Either way, I lose. If I kill him myself, she will cut me out of her heart. If she kills him, then she'll regret it for the rest of her life.

24

CELIA

I've taken to listening to the hand radio that Nic gave me before his first meeting. Sort of the way hobbyists listen to police scanners. The security team chatters on the radios all day, and I get some good gossip. It's how I learned which of the security guards has a crush on Sarah. And exactly how I will convince her to make me a cheesecake later.

I'm smiling into my book as I devise my plan. The library is quiet, and no one usually bothers me here except Nic. It's getting late in the day, and I'm surprised he hasn't hunted me down yet.

Things have been a little strained lately, between us stressing about each other's safety and the eventuality of what comes next.

Voices cut through the radio, and I try to focus as they talk over each other. It's a jumbled mess until one of the senior guards orders everyone to shut up and listen.

I can make out his gruff voice despite the static. "All men in position. Team one after Lucas, be advised, he's likely already lost to the enemy. Soo and Nic are hunting him now. Fucking idiot waltzed into a trap."

No. Maybe this is a training exercise? I sit upright from where I have been lying on the couch and race out of the room.

Nic isn't in his office or the bedroom. And I don't need to look further because, in my heart, I know neither he nor Soo are in the house.

Anger flashes through me. I throw open the closet door, find a pair of jeans, boots, and a jacket. Even as I curse him, I'm thinking about how upset Nic will be when he arrives home and doesn't find me here.

Yeah, almost exactly how I'm feeling right now. Why wouldn't he tell me he was leaving? No. I know the answer to this—because of what I'm about to do. And what I'll do next to stop my father from killing the last of the family I have left.

If my father took Lucas, there is only one place they will go, and there's no way Nic or Soo will know about it.

I sit on the edge of the bed and listen hard to the radio, trying to make out any more details. The voices sound mostly the same through the static, but I don't hear Nic's voice at all amongst the chaos.

Betrayal is a strange beast. If he finds my father, he'll surely kill him. Even though he promised me I could be the one to end my father's miserable life. I can't fault him for wanting to save his brother, my brother, but I also hate the thought that he can disregard a promise made to me so easily. Not that I believed for one second he meant to keep his word when the time comes. I've just always had hope that I can convince him in the moment.

So far, they aren't having any luck at my family's mansion; the guards think it's been mostly deserted—only a few staff members and my mother remain. Once they finish looking through the house and the garage, where will they turn? And how much time does Lucas have before my father gets bored with waiting on Nic to show up to save him? My father is a smart man, and no doubt, took Lucas to lure Nic into making a move before he's ready.

This is the exact reason Nic should have let me come along. He should have said something to me. I know how my father's fucked up mind works, and I know that no matter where my father goes, it will include a trap for those who come looking for him.

I can't sit around and wait any longer for my father to kill Lucas, or worse, Nic, when he walks into a trap.

Nic's office door is still open when I enter. It only takes a few seconds to hunt down some paper and a pen. Then I scribble out a note to Nic. It's not enough, not nearly enough, to explain how I feel about him—both my love and my hate. I hover the pen over the note and pause, unsure if I should reveal everything. What if I don't come back from this? It hurts me to think he wouldn't know.

I add a P.S. and wince as I write it, thinking about how angry he will be when he discovers it. Luckily, I'll be gone before that happens, and if I survive, he can punish me for it later.

I give it one last look before snatching the radio from where I'd set it on Nic's chair and lift the secret hatch to the safe.

It takes me a minute to remember the codes he wrote down for me. Once I get it open, I dig through it to find the keys to the basement door and the car that I know will be waiting at the end.

I study the safe contents one more time, my gaze lingering on the gun there. Finally, I snatch it out, close everything again, and march down the hall. The staff is still in the house, so I need to act like everything is normal, even as my insides are tied up in intricate knots.

Security is still chattering away, giving reports, and I'm still listening, hoping to catch Nic's voice amongst the rest.

I make it to the kitchen, and Sarah intercepts me. "Do you want me to set dinner in the dining room tonight, or do you want to take your food upstairs to eat until they get back?"

For a moment, I'm stunned, trying to organize my thoughts to give her some kind of answer, anything that will mean she remains without suspicion.

"I'll come back for it shortly. Just need to go do something."

I know it's a shitty answer, but before she can question me, I bolt past her toward the hall with the basement door. The lights are already on when I descend. It takes a few seconds to find the key to open the heavy door. Inside is a tunnel. It's rough stone and dirt floors, but there are lights built into the wall every so often, which I'm grateful for because my dumb ass didn't think about bringing a flashlight.

I don't know how long I walk. At some point, the radio's signal must have been blocked because it cuts out and goes silent. When I reach the end of the tunnel, there is another locked door to get through.

Just as Nic promised, a black SUV, like his security team uses, sits beyond the door on a sort of driveway that leads out of a large tunnel, which I assume is to the main road. If I'm trapped inside the compound, I have no doubt Nic will hear about it and come to deal with me instead of his brother.

I climb into the car that is way bigger than anything I've ever driven and give myself a pep talk as I set the radio in the cupholder. "You've got this. You've got this. You've got this," I repeat as I turn the key in the ignition.

Once I use the onboard maps to figure out where the hell the house is, I can easily map to the cabin in the woods my father ventures to at least once a month. It's the only place that makes sense for taking a hostage.

It's an hour's drive to get there, and as soon as I hit the main road, the radio comes back to life. The entire drive, I'm straining my ears for Nic's voice or news that they might have found Lucas, so I can turn around and go home.

Home.

When did Nic's house become my home? When I created a favorite spot on the couch in the library? When I learned to stock the good brandy in the pantry, and Sarah baked goods for me?

I glance at the wedding band on my finger and guilt claws at my insides. I promised Nic I wouldn't leave, and here I am, an hour away from our house, about to confront my father, to save my brother, all without backup. If I make it through this, I'm sure he's going to take a lot more than a belt to my ass as punishment.

I pull up outside the cabin. It looks old to anyone who might drive by, but the inside has been updated to rival a five-star hotel. There is one other vehicle here, and I can't tell if it's my father's or Lucas's.

I turn the volume down on the radio, tuck it in my pocket, slip the gun into the waistband of my pants, and climb out of the SUV—no use waiting in the car when Lucas could be dead at any moment.

The door is unlocked when I test the handle, which should have been my first red flag. The next one is the way the living room is eerily silent. I spot Lucas on the floor, belly down, blood caking his face and scalp. It looks like someone beat him to high hell, and I don't bother stopping the tears as they pour down my face.

"Lucas," I whisper, trying to lift his head and wake him up. He's a big guy, and I can't carry him out of the house. Even if I could, I'd never be able to get him into the car afterward.

"Wake up, Lucas. Wake up," I say. Of course, he doesn't because my life isn't that easy or lucky.

A shuffling sound behind me makes me freeze. Slowly, I turn my head to glance at what's behind me. My gaze falls onto my father standing there watching us. When he realizes it's me, his face turns glacial. The same look he gave me the night he told me my sister was dead.

"What the hell are you doing here?" he demands, stalking forward to snatch me up by the arm.

I jerk away but don't get far before he drags me back into his tight, painful grip. "Answer me, girl. What are you doing here talking to this bastard?"

"What do you think I'm trying to do, Daddy? I'm trying to save him. He might be dying. Did you do this to him?"

My father narrows his eyes. "You're with them. You're with—"

Realization dawns, and I know my life is about to get a lot worse for the immediate future. "Are you fucking both of them? Because you should know, one of them is your brother."

I rear back, again trying to get free, but he just drags me to a chair and tosses me at it. It occurs to me I should be afraid. For my life, and for Lucas's, and yet, I can't summon it, not with my cowardly father standing in front of me.

"You knew," I accuse. "You know Lucas is your son, and still you did this to him?"

"He isn't my son. He is a mistake. Something that should have never happened. Did you bring the other Diavolo with you?" he asks, spreading the curtains to peer out into the gathering darkness.

When I don't answer him, he marches back across the room and strikes me hard in the face. I glare up at him. "No, it's just me. I came alone."

"Stupid girl. You're dumber than I thought you were if you'd come in here like this." He shakes his head in disgust and swings around to kick Lucas in the belly.

I jolt upright and rush over, but he only grabs my neck hard in his hand and drags me back to the chair. "Move again, and I'll shoot you so you can't."

"Then stop hurting him. He doesn't deserve that."

"You don't have any idea what he deserves. You're just the same as his mother. A little whore who fucks anything with a cock. At least his mother had the smarts to stay away from me after she got pregnant."

I narrow my eyes. "The way I heard it, you raped her."

He moves fast despite his age. One minute I'm sitting on the chair, and the next, I'm flat on the floor with my cheek split open.

I roll over to lever myself up, but I can't see out of my right eye, and my head is spinning. Somehow, I hit it on the hardwood and didn't realize.

My father stands over me, staring down into my blood-streaked face. "You're just like all the rest. I had high hopes for you when you were going to marry that Gardello boy, finally worth the money spent keeping you alive all these years. But no, you had to go and blow it, and Diavolo too, I imagine."

Rage and anger have my adrenaline spiking, and my foot moves without thought. I kick out at his legs, but he neatly dodges them and returns one to my ribcage.

Pain shoots up my side, and I roll over, trying to protect my new wound.

He crouches down beside me and presses the muzzle of the gun to my forehead. "Tell me why I shouldn't shoot you right now and save myself some time when the other Diavolo finally arrives to save his brother?"

I won't justify my life to him for another second, so I keep my mouth shut and just glare my hatred toward him. How could this man have given me life?

He stares into my eyes, and I can see how lifeless and soulless his are, and I feel pity. But nothing else. He might have been my father when I was a young child, but it's been a long time since I've felt anything beyond duty toward him.

"If you need to kill me to feel like a man, then do it," I say. "But it won't change things. Nic is still going to kill you, eventually."

He curls his lip. "Nic, is it? So, you are fucking him."

A man in a black suit comes out of nowhere and ties my hands behind my back while my father continues to hold the gun to my head.

"Any last words," he says, stepping back to get a better angle, I assume.

I suck in a breath and brace myself for the shot.

25

NIC

I'm cursing Lucas all the way back to the house. Soo sits in the driver's seat, listening to me rant about my idiot brother the entire trip. We spent most of the afternoon looking for him once I got word he'd been taken. The spies Soo had on him spotted him rolling out this morning, and by the afternoon, Lucas had made a move and gotten caught.

How did one old man get the drop on my brother? He must have a lot of extra security right now. Maybe they were able to subdue him. But there weren't any signs of a struggle at the family house, and the wife was too drunk to do anything but stare at us while we combed her mansion. We left her there with her booze and the heavy sadness that seemed to stir in the surrounding air.

I took two seconds to look into Celia's old room. It had been cleaned out, completely empty of belongings and furniture.

Telling her how easily her family erased her from their lives would hurt her, so Celia will never know.

Once we get home, I go in search of Celia. She's not in the bedroom, and it's past dinner time. I check the library, then circle back to my office. On the desk is a piece of paper.

I scan the scribbled frantic handwriting and gently set the paper down on the desk. Soo walks into the room and sits down in the chair. But I'm already around the chair and out the door before he chases after me. "What's going on?"

"Celia went after him. She heard the news about Lucas on the security channel and obviously knows something about her father that we don't."

I spin in place a few times, cupping my head in my hands. "If he has her right now. I don't know where they are."

Soo takes my hands and drags them down so he can look in my eyes. "Stay calm. Throwing yourself into the fight without a plan will get you both killed. Think. Think about Celia. She needs you to help her, so think about what she's said to you in the past. Think about anything she's mentioned about her father even in passing."

I can't think around my heart pounding in my ears. Soo's voice breaks through some of it. I only catch a few snatches of words. "Think about what she said."

We have only talked about her father in the past. Since things grew warmer between us, we've been ignoring the topic because eventually, it will mean the end of something. I wrack my brain, forcing myself to focus around the rage, making a rising tide in my blood.

Soo fishes his cellphone out of his pocket and starts typing at a break-neck pace, even for him. When he curses loud and long, I finally pull out of the fugue. "What? Tell me you know where she is."

He holds the phone up and shows me a map. "She took the SUV outside the tunnel and programmed in the address to the destination. I know exactly where she is."

When he heads down the stairs ahead of me, I grab his arm. "No, I have to go alone. If something happens to me, or to Lucas, or to any of us, I need you here to take care of things. Make sure our business is handled."

Soo halts on the staircase, gaping at me. "You want me to stay here while you go save Celia and Lucas alone? Not a fucking chance."

I shove him hard against the wall. "What do you think Ricci will do if I roll up on his house with an army with me? He'll shoot them both and then come for me with his own small battalion."

"Fuck!" Soo shouts. No doubt hating this powerless feeling as much as I do.

I pass him and bound down to the foyer and out the front door. The SUV is still parked out front, and I send the security team inside to help Soo figure out how to proceed once I save Lucas and Celia.

The address is already programmed in the map, thanks to Soo texting it to the computer, and I pull away from the house.

It's an hour's drive to the lakeside place the map is taking me. A cabin? She had mentioned a cabin where her father liked to go fishing.

I can't focus on anything but the road as I drive, or I think up scenarios in my head about what he might be doing to her. And if he finds out what she actually means to me, fuck. He'll kill her just to mess with me.

My stomach rolls and twists, my fingers are tingly with adrenaline. I can't fuck this up, or I could lose everyone I love in one fell swoop.

I turn the headlights off when I make it to the side road that is supposed to lead to the house. It's smaller than what I would have expected, considering the mansion the bastard lives in. And I'd searched every inch of that house.

I climb out of the vehicle and tuck a gun into the back of my pants. No doubt he'll take it the moment I step in the door, but I prefer to be armed.

The only sounds I can catch are bugs and the soft slap of water against wood. I creep up the porch to the door and press my ear to the smooth wood.

I catch Ricci's raised voice, "Any last words?"

There's no time to consider my plan. I snag the gun from where I tucked it and move to bust through the door. But several sets of hands take hold of me from behind. I swing out, but others grab my arms and wrench the gun free.

I manage to take down one with a solid punch to the side of the head. More men charge at me, and after knocking the wind out of me with a sharp kick to my ribs, I'm burrowed into the corner of the porch, where they are able to overpower me.

A car pulls up behind mine, and several men pour out. All of them in full tactical gear carrying automatic weapons. Fuck, this isn't good.

Ricci throws the door open, casting light across the patio. "Ah, finally, my last guest. Come inside so we can speak properly."

"Fuck you!"

He laughs. The bastard who is holding my wife and brother hostage fucking laughs.

"Let them go, and you can have me. You can have my entire organization with it."

Celia screams from inside. "No, don't!"

There's a thud, and her voice cuts off. Ricci's shadow breaks up the pattern in the doorframe again. "Sorry, my daughter never knows when to keep her mouth shut."

I grit my teeth and punch one of the goons trying to hold me down. I'm rewarded with a right hook against my jaw. I revel in the pain, letting it fuel my anger.

"Bring him in," Ricci orders, and his men drag me inside the cabin.

Once we reach the door, Ricci retreats into the room. Two guards enter behind me and close the door with a heavy, final thump.

Lucas is lying on the floor across the room, his face swollen and bruised. Celia is sideways on the floor in the other area. Her face is pink from crying, there's a gash on her cheek, and her right eye is swollen. I will fucking kill this man if it's the last thing I do.

"You have me now, so let them go. Tell me what you want, and I'll tell my men to do it. You'll be the most powerful man in this state again."

Ricci waves his gun at the guards, and they reach up to wrench my arms behind my back to handcuff me. The goon sits me on a stool near the door, far away from Celia. She is laid on the floor, her hair pooling around her. My chest aches from looking at her. I want to raze this entire room and carry her home.

She meets my eyes, and hers are swimming with tears as she mouths the words, "I'm sorry."

I shake my head. Ricci looms closer now that I'm less of a threat to him. "Let them go," I order again.

As I suspected, he simply laughs, then brings the gun down into my face, splitting my cheek open with the butt of his handgun.

It's not the first time I've taken a gun to the face. I turn my head back to him, glaring. "Let them go," I say again, "or I'm going to choke the life out of you with my bare hands."

Ricci looks at me long and hard before bringing the gun down again, this time harder. Pain splinters under my eye, but I shake it off. But he doesn't like the fact that his blows are barely fazing me. He hits me again, this time on the side of the neck, then my temple, which shoots sparks through my eyesight.

"Stop!" Celia screams. "Stop hitting him, please!"

Ricci rounds on her, gun raised, like he might hit her again. She squirms away, right into the feet of a guard, who puts his hands on her to sit her up.

Once she's secure with the guard, Ricci brings his attention back to me. My eyes are on the guard, and the fucking grim look he's giving Celia sitting against his boot laces.

"Don't you fucking touch her," I say, making direct eye contact with the guard.

His smirk tells me what he thinks about my threats. I smirk back, even though my teeth are coated in blood. After I rip Ricci's head off, that fucking guy is next.

Ricci advances again and sits down opposite me. The look in his eyes promises murder, but the look in mine promises pure torture. I can't wait to get my hands on him. I'm buzzing with it.

"So, what was your plan? Get the other families to turn on me and attack once I'm vulnerable?"

I'm slow to answer, letting him seethe as he thinks I'm ignoring him. "As far as I can tell, you are vulnerable. I have what I need from the five families to ensure your power base is gone. Even if you kill me, that destabilization is already set, and I've already made sure things get carried out."

"Oh, I plan to kill you and your useless bastard brother. Then I'll move on to my whore daughter after I've let her watch you both die right in front of her. How does that sound?"

I shrug despite my bonds. "It sounds like a pleasant dream, Ricci. Hold on to it while you're able. Because soon, I'm going to make sure you have no dreams ever again."

There's movement by Celia, and I drag my eyes to the guard. He's kneeling behind her, a bunch of her hair in his hand, and he's sniffing it. Smelling her fucking hair right in front of me. I briefly wonder if he knows that he just signed his death warrant.

Glancing down at Lucas, I realize that my brother's eyes are open again. He is looking straight at me, giving me a single nod.

I shift on the seat to make sure I can at least stand. Ricci is droning on about something involving dismantling my territory, but I'm not paying attention, not while that fucking man is touching my wife.

My vision takes a red haze until I can almost no longer think straight. All I can see is his blood on my hands so I can keep her safe. Then I hear engines revving up in the distance, and I know this is my chance.

Backup is here.

I launch my head back and into the guard behind me, then headbutt Ricci in the same move. I hit him in the face hard enough to send him reeling backward into the door, his nose most likely broken. Ricci lunges for me, but I'm charging across the room at the guard. I ram my shoulder into his chest, using my entire weight, and we both go tumbling to the floor.

Out of the corner of my eyes, I see Lucas taking down one of the guards before untying Celia. All the while all hell breaks loose outside of the cabin. No doubt Soo and my men are killing every single person surrounding this place.

In the shuffle, Celia moved out of the way. Ricci trains his gun on me, but then I look over his shoulder and smile. Celia has her own gun pressed into the soft space under Ricci's ear.

"Drop your gun, or I will shoot you in the head." Her voice is clear and calm, and something warm and sweet blooms through the rage in my chest. Pride. I'm so fucking proud of her right now.

The man I'd shoved off her finally gains his footing, but she shakes her head at him. "Don't even think about it. I'll kill him before you get your gun out of your holster. And if you touch my husband, he'll be first, and you'll be next." There's a dark edge to her voice I've never heard before, but damn, my queen, as she stands up to these bastards, is incredible.

"Husband? I will admit I'm a little shocked, but not that much. He got what he wanted. Now I have to wonder, what do you plan to do here, Celia?" Ricci asks, his gun now on the floor by his feet. She uses her own foot to slide it out from in front of him and out of reach of the other guard. "I don't know, Daddy. This whore doesn't really make plans. I figure I'll go with the flow, kill the guy who annoys me the most, and then move to the next."

She stares at me over her father's shoulder. "Are you okay?"

I nod. "Need to get these cuffs off."

She motions to the other guard with the muzzle of the gun. "Unlock him and then step away slowly."

Ricci jerks in front of her, trying to create a distraction, but she doesn't fall for it. Instead, she presses the gun tighter into his neck.

"Now, Daddy, we are going to have a little talk."

26

CELIA

*M*y hand is shaking on the grip of the gun, and my palm is slick. When I grabbed it out of the safe, I didn't even think to check if it was loaded. So, my threats might get me killed. I'm just hoping they would have loaded the gun for the emergency safe.

I check on Nic. His face is bruised and swollen, but otherwise, he doesn't look like he's the least bit uncomfortable. Every bruise and scar he leaves with, I'm going to feel guilt over. I hate that he's here because of me.

"What are you going to do now, Celia? Are you going to shoot me in the head? Or let your husband do it?"

I'm so tempted to beat the shit out of him with the cold metal, just like he did to Nic. But I know he's trying to bait me, draw me into his little game so he can get inside my head. For some reason, he's always considered us women of the family beneath him, idiots, and not worth his time.

It's always hurt that he thinks that, even though I'm smarter than him. And for once, I have the opportunity to get some answers. "Why are you like this? What made you turn into this person? A man who treats his family like trash and goes around competing to be the evilest villain."

"Don't talk to me that way, girl. You are not my equal, and I don't answer to you."

Nic crouches in front of my father, his eyes scanning his features. "You're right. She's not your equal. She's so much better than you will ever be. You are absolutely nothing."

My father leans forward, and I tap the muzzle against his skin, reminding him I'm there and ready to blow his fucking head off.

I'm nervous with Nic so close to my father. But he doesn't do anything but stare him down, forcing him to meet his eyes.

My father shakes his head and spits at Nic's feet, but then he turns his head and speaks to me. "You would betray your own blood for this Costa trash? You're even more of a whore than their mother was."

My mouth falls open, and I stare between the two men who have created my entire world. "What did you say? Why did you say that name?"

Something evil flashes across my father's face. This time he's speaking to Nic. "She doesn't know, does she? You didn't tell your little wife who you really are? What name she now bears as her own?"

I hate he thinks he has something up on me, or Nic, but I can't process what he said in this environment. Until my father presses on with another revelation. "Don't you remember, Celia? You and this one used to play as children? He's the one who gave you that disgusting scar that made you almost useless to me as a bargaining chip for marriage."

I reach up and trace my fingers down the line on my face. My gaze jumping to Nic, trying to ferret out the truth there. He gives me nothing. His jaw is locked as he stares at my father. Completely unreadable. However, my father looks practically gleeful in his position between my husband and my gun.

He continues the conversation as if I'm participating. "Did you let him fuck you, and you didn't even know who he is?"

Bile rises in my throat, and I close my eyes for a heartbeat to get my bearings. It's not the fact that he is one of the supposedly dead Costa brothers, but because he lied to me all this time when he no doubt knew who I was when he kidnapped me.

"Since we are in the mood for confessions. Why don't you tell Celia what you did to my family when you decided you needed more power?"

My father looks smug as he bounces his gaze between us. "Why should I? You already know my sins, just as I know yours. What difference does confessing them make?"

Nic nods. "You're right. Let's just finish this." He turns his gaze back to me. "I'm sorry, Celia. I promise I will explain everything later, but right now, we need to end this. He is trying to get to you. Don't let him. He wants you dead, and he will kill you if he ever gets a chance."

Despite my anger toward him for lying to me, I agree with him. I don't want to believe my father would kill me, but I know it's true. I can see it in his eyes. Besides, he had no problem killing my sister for much less of an infraction.

Sensing my struggle, Nic steps closer. His arms come around me from behind, and he places his hands around mine, steadying my grip on the gun. His whisper against my ear shoots shivers down my spine. "I told myself when the time came, I'd do this for you. Take this burden from you, so you don't have to take this mark on your soul. But I can't deny you the justice that was denied to me. Kill him so we can go home."

I don't risk looking at his face, letting his solid presence surround me as I stare down the end of the gun at a monster. "Why did you kill her? Tell me that at least," I say, hoping for once in his miserable life, he'll do the right thing and tell me the truth.

"Your sister?" His eyes narrow, and a dangerous smile cuts across his weathered face. "Turns out she's not the only whore in the family; you're way worse. I should have started with you."

"But why did you kill her?" I scream. My voice breaking at the end.

"Because she defied me when she refused to marry the man I provided her. Your useless mother gave me two useless fucking girls, and you both had one job. Neither of you could do it."

A buzz is building in my head and along my limbs. Not a vibration but a feeling, a tingle, a demand to take this man's life and make him pay for all the crimes he's committed. The ones against me and my sister, the ones against Lucas and Nic, and probably countless others. How many lives had he destroyed during his reign over the five families? I fear speculating on the number.

A few heartbeats pass as I look into his eyes. There's no warmth in his gaze, nothing I recognize from the man I've lived with most of my life. I risk a peek at Lucas. There are no visible bullet holes and I sigh in relief.

Nic leans in and whispers in my ear. "You don't have to do this. I can take care of him for you."

I shake my head and square off with the gun again. No. I need to do this. I need to make him pay for everything he's done to me. Tears are pouring down my cheeks, and I don't bother wiping them away, especially not with the gun in reaching distance of my father.

"She's too weak," my father says to Nic or to no one; maybe he just likes to hear himself speak. "You think she'll be a good bride? She doesn't even have the stomach to take out a man like me. What if she has to make an actual difficult decision? She won't have the stomach for it, and you'll always be shielding her from the hard things."

My father turns to me next. "You won't do it. You're too weak. Your mother will be so ashamed of you. I can't wait to tell her both of her whore daughters are dead. Maybe she'll finally fall into that bottle for good and take care of herself before I have to put her out of her misery."

"Shut the fuck up," Nic snaps at him, and his grip tightens around mine. "Let me help you do this. I can help you pull the trigger if you need me to. I can do that for you."

"How fucking sweet," my father quips.

I glare at him, letting Nic align his body with mine, fit against me so I can lean into him. We have so much fucked up shit between us right now, but I can't deny whatever is between us has long passed a marriage of convenience or some sort of deal.

"Just a little pressure is all it takes. One shot, and he's gone and can never hurt you again. You can do this. You can avenge your sister, and my dead brother, and my family with one shot."

The absolute trust in his tone threatens to rip me open. I sob and then shake myself to clear my head again. A little pressure to end a monster who deserves it more than anyone I've ever met.

"Fucking weak. I'm ashamed you're my blood. Can't even fucking kill a man when you're pointing the gun point-blank at his skull."

Nic barks out next to my ear. "If you don't shut the hell up, I'm going to remove your limbs and then let her finish you off. She might have a conscience, something you will never understand, but I certainly have no qualms about cutting you up. How long do you think you'll last before you cry? Before you beg me to end your miserable life to put you out of your misery."

My hands are shaking as Nic verbally lacerates him. But then he steadies them carefully as it's a privilege to do so.

Nic whispers just for me again. "Give me the gun, *stellina*. You don't have to do this. I'll make sure he pays for his sins, and you don't have to feel any less for not being able to do it yourself."

I take a deep breath and just know that I can't. There's no world in which I can pull this trigger and take his life like this. He may be guilty and an asshole. And he definitely deserves to die, but I won't be the one who does it.

I just can't.

27

NIC

She can't kill her father, but I stand behind her and wait for her to realize it on her own. And when we get home, I'll tell her how proud I am of her for being able to stay above all this shit. Then I will tell her how much I love her, hoping that she feels the same. When I made that deal to make her mine forever, I never considered she might one day feel something like love for me, but now I want her to. It's never something I thought I deserved, not after the terrible things I've done over the years.

Maybe what I'm about to do will atone for my sins.

She gives me a slight shake of her head, and I take the gun from her. I aim it at Ricci's head, letting Celia step behind me. I don't want to drag this on any longer. I simply want to end this and take my family home. I pull the trigger.

Click. Nothing happens, so I pull it again and again. *Click, click, click.*

I drop the gun just as Ricci lunges forward. I brace myself for his attack, just to realize he isn't lunging for me at all but Celia.

My mind goes blank. He swings his fist toward my wife, but I'm faster. I tackle him and pin him to the floor. With my hands on him, I don't bother to stop the rage from rising, pushing out, so I'm punching him in the face. I hit him once, and again, and again until my knuckles are split from the blows against the bones of his face.

Celia is screaming at me from somewhere, but even her voice can't pull me out of this rage. Because right now, it's time to settle things between Ricci and me. It's time to make sure he pays for his sins and for everything he's taken from my family.

Her hands come down on my shoulders, but I shrug her off, not wanting her to get hurt, even as I straddle her father and pound my fists into his ruined face. It's bloody and bruised, same as my knuckles and my own face. He moans loudly and ragged, his breathing liquid-filled.

I stare down into the face of the man I've hated most of my life, and I know it's time.

Wrapping my hands around his neck, I squeeze. He immediately brings his hands up and wrings my wrists with his palms, trying to pry me loose, but he's frail and old and is no match for the strength in my grip.

I squeeze tighter, leaning in harder, cutting off the airflow. How many times have I imagined killing this monster? Never had I considered choking him to death, and somehow, I'm here.

Celia is crying behind me, but I can't bring myself to stop, not now. Not as the light leaves his eyes, and he chokes on the only air left in his lungs.

A few more heartbeats later, and he jerks underneath me, then stills, his hands slipping off my wrists to hit the floor next to his body.

I release my hold on his neck and sit back hard on the floor. The jolt jerking up my body, reminding me I've taken a beating.

I take my time, steadying my hands, letting the reality wash through me. Taking lives is not something I relish doing, but in this case, all I can feel is a sense of relief at this man being off the face of this earth.

But now I have to face his daughter, the woman I love, knowing that I killed him in front of her.

I drag my gaze to hers. She's still standing by her father's feet. Her hands crossed over her mouth like she's stifling a scream. She's no longer crying, but her face is wet, as is her T-shirt, with tears, blood, and sweat.

"Celia," I whisper.

She drags her eyes from her father's body to my face. And I brace to see the rejection there. I'd never hidden the fact that I'm a monster from her, but now, she's seen what I'm capable of firsthand. Knowing and seeing are different things.

But it's not judgment I see in her face, but sheer relief. Like she can finally take a full breath after years of being under his mental and emotional torture. And I don't doubt she'd suffered in silence in that house.

I want to reach out and bring her into my arms, but again, I fear her shoving me away, not wanting my hands on her after what I just did with them.

"I..." But there are no words for what I want to convey to her. Everything builds up in my chest that I've been shoving down for weeks.

She doesn't speak. Instead, she throws herself at me, half falling, half kneeling to get into my lap and into my arms. I wrap myself around her, pulling her so she is sitting across my lap as I clutch her tightly to me.

All I can do is suck in a breath, and somehow it feels like it's my first. That's how I know my life only begins today.

28

CELIA

*I*n the backseat of the SUV, I curl up in Nic's lap, mindful of his many bruises. Lucas is sitting beside us, his head tipped back and his eyes closed.

"Don't worry, the doctor is already waiting at the house. He'll be fine."

"He needs a hospital," I point out, but Nic is already shaking his head. "I promise, he'll have the same medical care at our house, maybe even better."

Knowing arguing about it is futile, I sigh and let my head rest on his shoulder. "Why did you come after me?" I whisper. "I wanted to save him, and keep you safe. But if you hadn't come, we'd probably both be dead. Thank you for coming after me."

He shakes his head, running his hands over my back and down the length of my hair. His touch feels so good, and the relief I feel that this is over is a solid weight off my shoulders.

"You don't have to be strong," he tells me. "You didn't have to do any of this. Lucas walked into a trap all on his own. We would have come to save him, but you shouldn't have been caught in the middle. I'm so sorry."

I pull back, but keep as much of our bodies touching as possible. "But now you're hurt. If neither of us had shown up here, you wouldn't have gotten beaten up."

"True, but I also wouldn't have finally gotten revenge and removed a monster from the world."

I look him straight in the eyes and say, "I love you, Nic. It's not just because I've loved you a little bit for my entire life, but because you've shown me in a short time how much love I can have if I just take it when it's offered."

He stares at me, dumbfounded, before clearing his throat. "I love you too, *stellina*. I've loved you for a long time."

His words wrap around me like a warm blanket. He loves me. I don't understand why he did the things he did, but I know it's true. He loves me.

"Why didn't you tell me who you were?"

"I'm not that boy anymore, *stellina*. I don't deserve to be a Costa."

"But you are, you and Lucas both."

Nic shakes his head slightly, closing his eyes before speaking again. "Do you remember who gave you that name? *Stellina?*

I Look at him with confusion. "No. When you first called me it, I thought it sounded familiar, but I couldn't place it. No matter how I tried."

"It was my mother. She loved you too, you know. She used to call you her little star..."

"Oh, my god. I remember now. And I loved her too."

"I failed her. I failed everyone."

"Nic, you were just a child. Now you are a man, and you can take your rightful place amongst the five families again."

"I've been telling him this for a while, but the idiot won't listen," Lucas comments from beside us.

"Shut up, Lucas, before I knock you out again," Nic huffs. "With your father gone, I need to call the other members of the five families and make sure they know there is no vacuum of power, and anyone trying to change the status quo right now will be handled the same way Ricci was."

I nod, understanding what needs to be done.

By the time we pull up to the mansion, I'm almost asleep. The adrenaline from the cabin wearing off has me exhausted and aching all over.

As promised, the doctor and even a nurse are waiting when we walk in. They set up some kind of home hospital in the living room and examine Lucas immediately.

We go to our bedroom, and Nic climbs into the bed. I hold on to his shoulders as he lies back on the pillows carefully. When he's finally settled, I get the first aid kit from the bathroom and clean his wounds.

He gawks at me like he is in awe while I methodically and gently rub warm water and antiseptic over his cuts and bruises. "Thank you," he whispers. "You're incredible."

I open my mouth to respond, but the door bursts open, and Sarah bustles in with some water and a sandwich. "I wanted to make sure you had something to eat. The entire staff is on edge downstairs. I don't know if I reassured them, but they are all going about their night routines now."

"Thank you, Sarah," I tell her, grabbing the tray from her. "But we really just want to go to sleep."

"Of course, I'll make sure no one disturbs you." She disappears as fast as she burst into the room, leaving Nic and me alone once more.

I finish cleaning up his wounds before going into the bathroom and washing up myself. By the time I get back, Nic is passed out on the bed, sleeping peacefully. Part of me wants to go downstairs and check on Lucas, but my battered body is too exhausted, and I know he is in excellent hands.

Crawling into the bed, I curl up beside Nic, placing my hand in his.

There are still many things we need to figure out, but right now, all I can think about is how happy I am to be here with him.

We're safe... and I'm home.

EPILOGUE

Nic

One month later

$\mathcal{K}$ eeping my voice low, I give my instructions to Soo. "Make the calls, tell them when and where we are meeting today, and ensure everyone knows where they stand on this. I won't tolerate anyone trying to defy me."

"Are you sure you want me to do this?"

I stare at my friend, who suddenly looks older and a little gray. He'd been more worried about me than he let on. "Yes, of course. I want you to handle it. You are the only one I trust with this."

"I know, but this is more important than anything we've done before."

I nod. He is right, of course. Taking back my rightful place as the head of the five families is the second most important thing I've done... making Celia my wife will always be number one.

"I trust you. Give me an hour, and we'll be downstairs, ready to leave. Make sure Lucas is ready as well."

"I'll take care of it," Soo assures me. "I also got a call from the rehab facility this morning, updating me on Celia's mom. She is doing well in the program and asking to set up a video chat with Celia this week."

"I'll let her know." I'm not completely on board with Celia having a relationship with her mother, not when she hasn't been a mom to her for so long, but I also recognize my wife's desire to have a relationship with her.

Soo leaves the room, and I turn my attention back to Celia, who has cocooned herself in the covers on our bed.

"Princess, I need you," I whisper, peeling the blanket away from her. I drag her into me and kiss her lips. Then I lick them and trail my mouth down her neck. "I need to feel your naked body," I whisper into her skin. "I need you right here beside me with nothing between us."

"I'm here," she protests even as she arches her body along mine in invitation.

"Thank fuck, because if you were anywhere else, I would tear the world apart."

Her eyes flash open to meet mine. "Why?"

"Because you belong to me. And I love you, in case it wasn't crystal fucking clear."

Tears rim her eyes. "Hearing you say that never gets old."

"I love you more than anything in this world. I always will. You're my queen, *stellina*, and I'll stand in front of a thousand bullets for you."

"Please don't." She laughs. "I have to tell you something before you sacrifice yourself for me."

"It can wait." I tug her hand down to the waistband of my pants. When she protests, trying to free her hand from mine, I catch it and place it back over my already swelling cock. "No, princess. You're mine to take when I want, and right now, I need you too much to care about anything else."

She looks like she wants to argue with me, but I catch her mouth in a quick kiss. Not enough to hurt her, just enough to warn her. She moans into my mouth as my tongue meets hers, but breaks the kiss suddenly.

"I'm pregnant," she blurts out.

My mind goes blank. Utterly blank. For a long moment, I simply stare at her, forgetting everything, including my name and how to breathe.

"Are you okay?"

"Did you just say pregnant?" I ask, when I finally find my voice again.

"Yes. We're gonna have a baby." She smiles ever so shyly. "Are you okay with that?"

"*Okay*?" Is she kidding right now? "Just when I thought I couldn't love you anymore, you tell me you're giving me a child."

"So, you are happy, then?"

"I'm more than happy. In a few hours, the five families will officially announce me as their leader, and now you are telling me my queen is already carrying an heir to our empire. There is only one more thing that will make this day absolutely perfect."

"Does it involve your dick being inside of me?" She giggles.

"Damn right, it does."

~

Thank you for reading Devil You Know!
Preorder our upcoming release Hell, which is part of the Black Heart
series Heaven and Hell.

ABOUT THE AUTHORS

J.L. Beck and C. Hallman are an USA Today and international bestselling author duo who write contemporary and dark romance.

For a list of all of our books, updates and freebies visit our website.

www.bleedingheartromance.com

BLEEDING HEART ROMANCE

CASSANDRAHALLMAN
AUTHORJLBECK

CASSANDRA_HALLMAN
AUTHORJLBECK

CASSANDRAHALLMAN
JLBECK

Printed in Great Britain
by Amazon

75522968R10144